Prologue

I used to be a lot better at this. Speaking in front of people has always come naturally to me. Ever since things all got sorted out, I've been much better; worlds better. I guess it doesn't make it any easier that I'm trying to speak at a funeral; even more so that it's for one of the few people I loved more than anything. You.

They say there are three ways to make a person's soul shine; sing with them, dance with them, or laugh with them. I would watch your soul beam when you sang with me; it was one of your favorite things to do. I'd do all three and turn the world upside down just to see yours shine one last time, but some things in this world don't make sense, and that's okay.

"Friends. Family," I paused. It's hard to get words out passed a heart full of tears. I took a deep breath, and tried again.

"Family. Friends. I'm glad you all could make it." I stopped again; and looked at you. I stared at you. And then stared at you. And then stared at you; waiting for you to wake from your eternal slumber, kiss me on the cheek, and ask me to sing you your song. No such luck. At least we were able to do an open casket, but seeing your peaceful, pale, angelic face, I couldn't handle it. And then I lost it.

I couldn't hold back any longer. I'd held on for so long, but everyone has a breaking point, and I'd finally reached mine. With a final look back to the crowd, behind eyes drowned in tears and a face as red as a broken heart, I threw a hand up, mumbled a thank you under my breath, attempted to bear the best fake smile I could muster, and politely excused myself from the podium.

In this world, there are things we can fix and things we can prevent. But then there are a plethora of those where neither apply, and that's okay.   There's nothing we can do to change it, all we can do is cope with it.   Humor is my passion; it's what I do.   Not when it comes with such a heartbreaking situation, so I guess I have to find another way to cope.   You can only tell yourself it's not your fault enough times before the phrase loses merit and its meaning becomes useless.

Someone once told me this: "Sometimes, the world doesn't make sense; it just doesn't make sense. So many terrible, cruel things happen that we can't seem to wrap our minds around. That taxing, simple question repeats over and under in our minds: Why? Why? Why did it have to happen? Why did it have to happen to me? Why? While it may not be clear to you today, I can guarantee if you reflect on any disaster you've experienced in the past, you can link the chain of events that leads to something great that came out of it. Everything has its place in the universe. I promise you this much: Life can be hard. Life IS hard, but if you seek to find the silver lining, the world becomes a much less scary place. It may be hard to dance in the rain sometimes, but just look for the sunshine behind the clouds; rainbows are a symbolic reminder that even in the darkest of thunderstorms, something beautiful is waiting for us on the other side."

1

Let me paint you a picture: A quiet town.   A peaceful neighborhood.   A perfect subdivision.   A street ending in a cul-de-sac.   A house at the far end of the loop.   A two story house, colonial style, with vibrant vinyl siding in a beige tone, indicative of new construction; this was the vibe from the entire subdivision.   A tall standing oak on the right side of the house looking out, with an enormous cloud of green leaves encapsulating the top; singing, dancing, and laughing with the wind.   A beautiful green turf coupled with beds of flowers outlining the foundation of the house.   A crisp blue sky with enough clouds throughout to count on one hand.   Rays of sunshine covering every inch, transforming the portrait from wonderful to immaculate.

Now let's take a step inside.   Aromas of a home-cooked meal and cinnamon & spice scented air fresheners bombard the nose.   A family room to the left, dining room to the right, a kitchen past that to the left, and a living room & bathroom out of view, leaving the first floor revolving and open.   Marigold, lavender, and periwinkle shades reflect off the walls and decorate the atmosphere, along with pictures; a typical husband, wife, daughter showcase.   Upon shelves sit messages of a tender and inviting domicile; "Home sweet home," "This house is filled with love," and the like.   Exotic hardwood floors stretch from wall to wall and create a warm welcome up the stairs.   A magnificent, elegant banister accents the floor in white on the left, and back to a wall of color on the right.   On the second floor, a child is playing in one of two bedrooms. Then there's the study and a master bedroom which is equipped with another bathroom, the master bathroom, giving its occupant easy access to late night requests of nature. The master bedroom; a place of relaxation, concentration... and deception.

Back in the dining room is the image of a committed marriage in shambles.   A woman's defeated expression sits on top of a rolled and tattered posture, leaning against a set of granite counters separating the dining room from the kitchen.   Her elbows are pitted against her stomach and her hands are guns blazing, tips resting against her temples.   She's wearing a pastel yellow robe wrapped tightly at her waist by a matching belt and slippers.   Her long black hair is jostled, adding definition to her defeat.   And there's a man's head buried in a set of hands, supported by elbows resting on the dining room table.   A collection of tears begin to puddle on the cherry wood, along with a collection of thoughts running through my head. I don't know how it happened.   I don't know where I went wrong. But I'm determined to find out…

"I want a divorce."

The words resonated throughout the room.   Did I really mean what I was saying?   Those wedding vows —that, "'til death do us part" — that has to stand for something, has to mean SOMETHING… doesn't it?   Does it?

"Can't we go see someone? I think counseling would be really good for us.   For Jellybean!" she said.

"A counselor?   What good is that going to do us?   You cheated on me with one of your clients in our own bedroom!   You couldn't have done that at his place?"   What was I saying?   Was I condoning this?   Was I subconsciously aware of what she's been doing all this time and just choosing not to see it?…   "All this time?" I don't know how long this has been going on, how could I possibly think "All this time?"   How long HAD this been going on?

"How long has this been going on?"   I mumbled; the question I dreaded to ask, and feared the answer to.   It was hardly a question so much as a thought that accidentally spilled out of my brain, into my mouth, down my tongue, and died impatiently off my lips.

"Is that important?" she asked.

"Am I important?" I sneered back.

"Of course you are.   We've just been going through a rough patch, and you just… and I…"   Her voice trailed off.   She didn't know what she was saying.   She didn't care.   She COULDN'T care! How could she?   Cheating is the most disrespectful thing someone can do in a relationship; and, no less, in our own bedroom!   Where I lay my own head!

"I want a divorce." I repeated.

"We can work through this.   We can get passed this together! I know you're angry right now, but we can do this!   You, me, and Jellybean, we'll get passed this!"

Jellybean... The name made sense to me this time. My little Jellybean; the best thing that ever happened to me. Four years old and not a care in the world; a happy-go-lucky one, was she. In fact, someone had a birthday coming up; in fifteen short days. You remember. I lived for that little girl. I would've died for that little girl; that's hard to swallow. I thought my wife felt the same way. Now, Jellybean seems like nothing more than a weapon at her disposal to make this marriage work.

"You cheated on me! How could you do that?" I asked.

"I don't know!" she insisted.

"Why did you do it?" I continued.

"I just... don't know."

Our words started to blend together. It was much less an argument than a conversation with myself and her just forcing out automatic responses to put me at ease that I wasn't just having a conversation with myself. We were getting nowhere.

"So, what do you want to do?" she inquired after an almost awkwardly long pause.

"I guess we can try to go to counseling," I agreed.

"We don't have to go if you don't want to."

"Of course I don't want to. I also didn't want you to cheat on me, but that obviously didn't work out in my favor."

"I understand that you're upset with me, but you don't have to come down on me like that."

"Come down on you?! Honey, you shared the one thing that is supposed to be exclusive to us! You took him to my room, my domain! Do you not understand how repulsive that is?"

"I do!" she retorted. "It's just so hard! You live in your own head! You're so disconnected! I don't know what to do anymore! I'm miserable! I feel like you don't love me! I feel…" she trailed again. She always does that. She never expresses her feelings. I have to force it out of her, and even then, it's like she's not always completely open.

"We'll do the counseling thing. If that doesn't work, we have to figure out who gets the house, what happens with Jellybean, all of that," I explained.

"Well, we won't have to do that. We'll get it figured out," she replied.

"I'll see if I can set up an appointment for tomorrow."

"I love you."

"I… just, give me some space." She was suffocating me. In the past 10 years of our marriage, I haven't felt more constricted than I have in the past two. She always wants to know every little detail. Where I'm going, where I've been, who I'm talking to on the phone, how my day went; she was never like this before! What happened to her in the past two years?

Work was quite a burden to bear with such a disruption of thoughts running through my mind. If I were to be diagnosed as being clinically depressed, this was a parallel depression, unmatched by any prior feelings of loneliness or being "down." Sitting at my desk, I wasn't really sitting at my desk; my head was somewhere else. Playing a soundtrack of endless questions stuck on repeat was my mind, regarding the "who's," "why's," and "how's" of this predicament. Who exactly was he? Why did she do it? How did I let this happen? Was it my fault? Of course it wasn't my fault! I didn't throw her at him! She did this to me! I didn't do this to myself! But, God dammit, I need answers! My fists rattled my cubicle as they met my desk, pens swilling, my monitor cowering, but then patiently staring back at me. A few heads peered into my space in curiosity.

I put my head down in complication, and then I realized my coffee mug was on its side and rivers of brown were bleeding down my paperwork. Great. I scooped all of the files from my desk into the wastebasket, swore to myself, and started my search to refresh the numbers and equations I lost. Back to square one. I can't go on like this. I'll go crazy before I get any better! A counselor won't work. But it's my only option. I could... kill myself. That would solve all my problems. No more worries; no more complications. Isn't that what I'm looking for? Isn't that my best option?

"No." A woman's voice broke my deep pattern of thought. But, odd, I looked around my vicinity and found no face to match what I just heard. That was either a coincidence, or my mind is playing tricks on me...

"What?" I asked. Still nothing; must've been a coincidence. My mind rattled and retorted continuously for what seemed like hours, but couldn't have been more than twenty minutes. I glanced at my wrist and the hands on my watch confirmed my assumption.

"For the third time, I need you in my office," my boss peered at me.   The third time? Where was I for times one and two? At any rate, he sounded frazzled.   It was probably just my own projection. There's a concept in psychology about types of defense mechanisms where you unconsciously project your own undesirable behaviors onto someone else to reduce anxiety, give reason to inexplicable feelings, and redirect fault.   I was frazzled.

The conversation in his office went something like this: words, words, words from him; obedient head nods from me.   More words; more head nods.   A head shake here, an empty promise there, and a few more words followed by a polite dismissal.   The topic of discussion?   I have no idea.   Between all of the thoughts of my personal situation, there was some talk of how the company's doing, where it's headed, what's expected of me, and my memory ends there.

That's not important anyway.   What's important is that my marriage, my mind, my life is in limbo right now, and I need to get it straightened away.   Our first counseling session is tomorrow, so I need to get the hell out of here, get a good night's sleep—or as good as I can get with a brain in overdrive—and wake up ready to tackle all of the complications and conundrums that will come of these sessions.

2

Falling asleep was, of course, no easy task. Tossing and turning; turning and tossing. Thinking and thinking; thinking and thinking. At this point, I'm just beating a dead horse, but at this point, I'd rather be the horse. Maybe I'm just thirsty. Maybe getting a drink will occupy my brain for a nominal two minutes. Whatever; two minutes of sanity.

The kitchen was dark; dimly lit by the cliché moonlight reaching in from the window. Only the parts of the room touched by the moon were illuminated, contrasted by pure darkness, leaving a black and white abstract painting on my visual palette. Quite the somber view for quite the somber mood.

My legs, set to autopilot right from my bed, had found themselves in front of my fridge, glass in hand, waiting for it to take the reigns and activate the water dispenser so I could dissolve my dehydration & anxiety and resume—initiate, rather—my slumber.

I'm usually a "glass is half full" kinda guy, but right now, this glass is definitely half empty. I tipped my head back and emptied the water into my mouth as it chased its way down into my uneasy stomach. Ahh. I left my head tilted, closed my eyes, and let out a sound of satisfaction.

I came back to the world and twisted my head toward the bathroom; the medicine cabinet. Maybe a few sleeping pills as assistance to my problem that would prove exhausting if gone unresolved? Maybe a handful as assistance to my sweet release from this torture that's been created for me in my mind. Just as this agonizing relief crossed my mind, something else caught the corner of my eye. A silhouette. A person? Someone watching me? In my house? "Who the fuck is that?" I shouted reflexively. Well, there are other people in this house. You're being irrational. But it was too large to be Jellybean. And too, fluid, to be... human. More irrational. It was in my head. I'm tired and have a ton on my mind. Clearly it's taking revenge by playing tricks on me. That's logical. Back to bed I go.

I made a pitstop to the bathroom and limited myself to just a couple sleeping pills; I needed to take the edge off. I knew that with the way my mind was going, I'd never get any sleep. With the cap clasped between my fingers, I tilted the bottle and let a few tablets tumble onto my palm. I threw my hand up to my face and the tablets shot to the back of my mouth. I chased them down with what was left of my water. I stood in silence for a moment before I heard the hardwood floor creaking beneath footsteps in the living room.

"Babe?" I called out. Babe. What a joke. I laughed to myself. There was no call back, so I walked lightly with caution back to the kitchen, keeping a close watch on my surroundings as I went.

No signs of life down here; I really just need to get to bed. I made it to the kitchen sink and gently placed my empty glass in it. I spun around, rested my palms on the edge of the sink and took in my house and everything that had just transpired. Were those really just goings-on in my head? Or is somebody in here and I just don't see it? I was too anxious to be scared really.

"If there's someone in here, just kill me now," I said to the refrigerator. And if you're a ghost, take me away to your mystical island of the lost and the hurt. A secluded place where the depression dogs and the monsters of anxiety roam free. I laughed to myself again.

"Please, just take me away, whoever you are," I whispered under my breath. On that note, I shook the thoughts and desires from my head and pushed myself out of the kitchen and back up the steps.

Retreating to my room, I laid my head on the comfort of my pillow, and gazed up at the ceiling. My mind wouldn't shut off, so I closed my eyes to give it one less thing to process. That shadow in the corner of my room was hurting my eyes anyway; like a blinding light. It took a minute before it hit me: That's strange; why would a shadow hurt my eyes like a bright light? Shadow? Silhouette? That figure's in my room now?! My body jerked upright and rested on my hands as my eyes darted open and around the room all in one swift motion. The dark... whatever that was is gone now. And then suddenly I became uncontrollably drowsy; my eyes too heavy to hold open. My arms grew weak and collapsed, forcing my body back onto the bed. I was in a losing battle against my eyes to open them back up. I fought and fought and a moment later, opened them with no effort at all. I found myself laying down. On the sand. On a beach. By myself.

3

You always loved art, as much as I loved seeing you smile. So, let me paint you another picture. There's an island, with no real color. It's not black and white; more like grayscale. If you look hard enough, you can make out subtle hints of color, but mostly just dull, dull grays and then grays. The sky's suffocated by an array of clouds in an assorted, yes, gray. There's not much vegetation here, an occasional patch of beach grass and sea oats; all flora, no fauna. Other than that, just random giant boulders, sea stacks strewn about, and sand as far as the eye can see.

The ocean is continuously crashing it's way onto shore, but, oddly enough, it's only identified by witnessing its action. There's no sound to the waves. In fact, there's really no sound at all; just an eerie silence that washes over the ears. THIS is a parallel depression.

I don't know what I'm doing here; I'm not even sure whether or not this is reality, but there's no use just standing here. As I start walking, I realize that I'm barefoot, but I can't feel the sand beneath my feet. I must be dreaming. The slow, gentle breeze off the shore brushes against my five o'clock shadow and argues otherwise. I walk to the edge of the large boulder I had apparently been walking on and come to a set of stairs carved right into the rock.

As I descend the stairs, I notice a door about fifteen feet in front of me. That's odd, just a door, out in the open, fixed to nothing, but standing as though it was. It piques my interest, so I try the handle and am surprised to find it locked from the inside, or my side, rather. I twist its lock, turn the deadbolt, and give it a second try. The handle agrees with me this time, but I pause before I open the door. What's on the other side? What COULD be on the other side? Whatever this island is, there's obviously nothing that should keep me from going through this door. Unless this is one of those crazy dreams where I open the door and walk through into a completely different scene. Nevertheless, I let out the breath I had been holding in and made the pass through the doorway.

What laid on the other side was... nothing. Well, not nothing exactly; just the rest of the island. And a person standing about two football fields away straight ahead and slightly to my right. Whether it was fear-induced adrenaline or pure curiosity, I don't know, but something took control of my feet and sauntered me in the direction of whoever, WHATEVER that was.

I took note that the wind was still hugging my face at every moment, but strange now was the quiet whirring sound it was whispering in my ears. And it seemed that as I closed the gap between this figure and me, my ears began to pick up another audible range that could only be described as the crashing waves that I couldn't hear at first. Still far too quiet to be sure, but it's the only thing that makes sense.

Now that I was closer, I could make out her features. She wore a white evening dress that came halfway down her calves.   She had long black hair that was covering her face on account of the wind. I couldn't tell if she was tall or short as I wasn't close enough yet. She was turned partially to her left, playing with her dark hair in bouts of casual controlled rhythm. And she was a she. There was no questioning that; at this distance, that wasn't a visual certainty. Something inside me confirmed it.

At about fifty yards away, I could see she was almost glowing. Not in a divine kind of way, but more in an incandescent, trivial kind of way; almost shiny. She must've put on suntan lotion in the hopes of soaking up some sun. She must've thought she was going to a different beach. A seasoned thief couldn't steal any sun rays from this scene.

Once I was right in front of her, time seemed to stop. The waves paused, the wind ceased, and I was stopped in my tracks. She turned and gazed at me, almost through me. But something about her eyes... My wife's eyes. She had my wife's eyes. In fact, she resembled my wife; like a sister she never had or... I don't want to think about that. Suddenly, as the world was coming back to me, I could hear traffic, and she pushed me away from her with a minor pump to my chest with the palms of her hands as she said, "Wake up." And then I did.

4

My eyes jolted open and took in the new world around me. I was no longer on the island, nor was I in my room. I wasn't even in my house. Standing alone, still a little dazed as my surroundings slowly made sense in my head, I was about a quarter mile down the street from my house. I was standing on the curb of a major road we live by. Startled by either the traffic that honked at me as I stood a few feet from a hospital visit or the fact that I wasn't in my bed in the comfort of my home, my heart was racing.

How the hell did I get here? I was still in my pajamas with no shoes on my feet. It's like someone put me here. My dream; that woman pushed me right before I woke up. Had she somehow saved my life by pushing me backward before I woke up? Was that push the reason I woke up in the first place? Was I sleepwalking? So many questions; and so much on my mind as it is. The proverbial hamster running the wheel of my brain had keeled over and died at least ten times by now.

I have to put the events of tonight into the back of my mind. I need to focus on what lies immediately ahead; counseling, my future with my family, my future. I quietly, but casually, walked back into the house through the front door to find my wife nestled peacefully, but concerned, on the couch. She had been sitting on the edge with her elbows resting on her knees and her face resting in her hands. Without moving, she asked, emotionless, "Where were you?"

"Oh, you're suspicious of MY whereabouts?" I sneered. "Don't worry about me; just go to bed."

"I was just worried about where you were. I'm just making sure you didn't die. Why must everything be an argument with you?"

"Nope; didn't die. Here I am. What a stupid thing to suggest. I'm fine. I'm not doing this now; it's four in the morning. I'm tired. I just want some rest before our wonderfully pointless rendezvous with our therapist. That's it; end of discussion."

She let out a huge sigh of surrender and stood up. "I need some fresh air," she informed me.

"Great," I replied, "and I'm going to bed."

I took a quick detour to the bathroom before heading back up to my bedroom. As I came back around the corner and began up the stairs, I placed a hand on the newel post and stopped. The air; there was something in it that played with my senses. It's been said that olfactory memories, that is memories based off of the sense of smell, are the most fervent triggers in our vault of memories, more notable than visual or auditory cues. It was... summer breeze; and roses. That's a painful memory to fathom, given my current situation.

But, as quickly as it came, the aroma shifted to another I didn't care to take in. It was rather faint, but rather evident as to what it was I smelled; cigarette smoke. My wife is smoking again? I crept over to the crack in the doorway to confirm my suspicions. I glared at the back of her head for a moment, waiting for her to turn around so I could see the cigarette in her mouth. I had to see it to know it was, in fact, true. Although, what good has my vision done me in the recent past? I feel like I've been going out of my mind with what I've been seeing, not to mention everything else that's been going on.

Amidst this thought, I saw it: she was still facing away from me as a smoke trail of white curls and twists danced away from the top of her head like a chimney stack. She did indeed pick smoking back up; one lie after another. I don't know if I can mentally handle another lie, another deceit, another tribulation. I need a drink. Maybe tomorrow.

My head naturally slung low on the way to bed. To say I was exhausted is an understatement. I was beyond it, beyond drained, beyond worn out; closer to enervated. Can't this just be over? As my head crashed into the pillow, sleep almost came naturally to me this round.

Nothing else out of the ordinary happened that night. Those sleeping pills certainly did their job this time around; almost too well. I don't remember having any other dreams; if I did, they were nothing notable or spectacular. Just peaceful, fruitful rest.

The air throughout the house the following morning found itself saturated with a deafening silence. Perfect. I took this opportunity to research sleepwalking on my laptop. I hadn't done that in a long time, sleepwalking; not since my grandfather had passed away years ago. Seemed like every time I had gone through something traumatic, my body liked to react this way.

Digging into my investigation, I found this to be somewhat true. Sleepwalking, or parasomnia as it's more professionally referred, is linked to both depression and stress; guilty and super guilty. This seemed to be quite accurate, considering I hadn't had any issues since my grandfather, with whom I'd been very close. It was my body's way of coping. My conscious body preferred alcohol, which is why I mostly stay away from it, but that's another tale for another time.

I continued reading the article and came to find out that parasomnia isn't just limited to sleepwalking. Parasomnia can refer to any type of activity you do while you're in the less-than-conscious: walking, talking, eating, even cooking can happen while you're out cold. I think the list is exhausted at that point, I can't imagine anything else you could do while you're sleeping.

Amid my self-issued curriculum and homework assignment, I stumbled upon, and learned about, another phenomenon. Lucid dreaming, the act of dreaming and being consciously aware you're doing so, is a coping mechanism for those suffering from anxiety. Furthermore, in lieu of the knowledge that you're dreaming, many people note that within the dream they can in fact control it. Not all lucid dreamers suffer from anxiety, but most all who do take relish in the ability to control the dream; a means to, in turn, control their anxiety, which is essentially a sense of feeling uneasy with a loss of control. A feeling of no control in this world; the command of total control in another. This makes perfect sense to me. This whole cheating fiasco has put my anxiety through the roof, in turn causing me to have a lucid dream on an island. Being able to completely control the world in my head, put my anxiety at ease, and however sleepwalking relieves depression, my body had done just that.

Except that it didn't work. I was still at an incredible unease; no amount of control of a dream in my head or an unconscious walk through the park will make me feel any better. And now among anxiety, depression, and a sense of total helpless- and worthlessness, I can now add utter confusion to the roster. What happened last night? Who was the woman from my dream? Did she actually push me clear of traffic and save my life? So many unanswered questions, and I had barely even begun to scratch the surface.

I guess it's safe to say I had felt a little better digging into lucid dreaming and sleepwalking. I use the term "better" VERY loosely. One small fraction of my entirely disheveled world was sorted out and organized; and brought on a whole new array of questions. The best thing for me to do at this point is to put what happened at the back of my mind as best as I can and focus on getting through my—our—first therapy session. Shit. Easier said than done.

"Ready to go?" she asked me.

"Yeah." I opened the closet door and grabbed a light jacket off of its coat hanger.

"Can you grab an umbrella? It's supposed to rain later."

"Got it," I said, reaching down to the bottom of the same closet to grab the umbrella. "Wow. This is the most normal conversation we've have in a pretty long time," I said sardonically.

"Yeah," she chuckled.

"That's not funny," I corrected her, "That's sad."

"Why do you always do this? You always…" I stopped listening. I had grown far too tired of her voice far too long ago. I just let her rattle on until she ran out of things to say halfway through our car ride.

After a long silence, I said, "Well, this should be pretty fucking fun."

She painted an "eat shit and die" look on her face, sent it over my way, and then turned and stared out the window the rest of the trip. Ah, sweet silence, how I've longed for thee.

5

"Where do you work?" the therapist asked impatiently, as though he'd reiterated the question multiple times. He shook me out of yet another deep spell of trainwreck-grade thoughts. His words startled me to reality as I shot a look in his direction and stared at him, hollow and blank. His words ran over in my head a number of times before they made sense to me. His eyes widened in an attempt to non-verbally ask me just one more time.

"Beta-Leaf Enterprises," I finally uttered.

"And what is 'Beta-Leaf Enterprises'? What does their business comprise of?" he interrogated.

"That's our business," I chuckled, first out loud and then to myself. "My boss," I began. I was going to say, "My boss always says that," but when I glanced at the therapist, I realized he wasn't amused, so I straightened myself in my chair. "It's an investment firm. We deal mostly with incredibly wealthy, that is to say upper class, folks who trust us with their money so we take it and invest in stocks, bonds, trusts…"

"I got it," he cut me off. Prick. "What do you do there?"

"I'm a clerical worker, essentially."

"You're a paper pusher?" he mocked. He stared at me hard, and waited, so I continued slowly, ignoring his attempt to belittle me

"I'm pretty much in charge of records: any time someone makes a transaction, I file it. When we get a new client, I file his paperwork. When…" He threw a "stop sign" hand up, catching me off guard. I stared at him, baffled, as he jotted a few notes down in his journal, or whatever it was.

He looked up when he was finished and met my wife's attention with a smile. "And how about you, dear? What kind of bread do you win?"

"Dear?" I thought I repeated audibly. Apparently I didn't, though, because their focus on one another didn't shift a degree.

My wife chuckled and blushed. "Oh, I'm just a masseuse," she divulged to her hands, which were fidgeting anxiously in her lap.

"Are you an independent contractor or do you work for someone?"

"Yeah, she works for Happy Endings & Hospitality," I blurted out, which forced my eyes to roll back into my skull.

The therapist's gaze pierced right through me, like he was trying to read the writing on the wall behind me; if looks could kill. Once he got his point across, he shot that oh-so-charming smile back in my wife's direction. "Sweetheart?" he asked. Sweetheart? Dear? This guy was testing my patience.

"I guess I'm an independent contractor," she explained. "I work out of my home."

"Ha!" I couldn't control myself. It was like someone took the reigns of my brain and pulled them in their own direction. Someone was pulling the strings of me, the marionette. "She 'works' from home," I ridiculed as I made air quotes with my hands.

My wife fixed a repulsive glare onto my person and the therapist fixed a repulsing hand onto her knee. "Please; I'll handle this," he said in a whisper as though I couldn't hear him.

"If you're gonna continue…" he started. He instantly became a TV show on mute. His lips were moving, but no words were escaping them. I got tunnel vision that filtered out everything else that existed in the world except for his ugly fucking face. The world was red; my vision was red. I was seeing red. It took every ounce of energy I had in my body to not wind up and punch him square in his ugly fucking face. Who the fuck does he think he is putting his hand on my wife like that? And the flirting? Sweetheart? Dear? My mind was racing again. I couldn't control myself; I needed to leave before I did something I'd regret. I needed to go back to what makes me comfortable. I needed… yes.

"What the fuck?!" I cut the therapist off with a roar. "Are you fucking kidding me?" And that was it; with that, I stood up and charged out the door. The last thing I remember was a look and posture of cowering fear frozen in them both; their hands stuck at their chests like a lion had just pounced in their direction.

The car ride was over before it started. My mind was too consumed; preoccupied. If my heartbreak wouldn't kill me, my anxiety sure as hell would. The scene at the therapist's office just kept playing over and over and over in my head. Sweetheart, Honey, hand on the knee. Sweetheart, Honey, hand on the knee. Sweetheart, Honey, hand on the knee. The world was in fast-forward as I made my way to the bar; as I said, the car ride was over before it started. But the nighttime world was in slow motion at the same time as I counted every rain drop that landed on my windshield. It was the only thing to do to keep my mind off of my anxiety, but my mind was everywhere: 1, 2, 3 raindrops. Sweetheart, Honey, hand on the knee. Did he say Honey? Or did he call her Dear? I was so frazzled, I couldn't recall. 4, 5, 6 raindrops. Sweetheart, Dear. Hand on the knee. Did it really matter, though? Everything that transpired in that room was wildly inappropriate and my actions were justified. 7, 8, 9 raindrops. Sweetheart, Honey. And so on. And then I pulled into the parking lot of Via 734. It was a pretty decent bar/nightclub downtown. Of course it wasn't very busy at all on an off night. Perfect, I just needed a few drinks to clear my head.

I walked in and it was your pretty typical Class A nightclub look: exotic hardwood floors; faux rock wall panels lining the walls from chair rails to the ceiling and eggshell black from the same chair rails to the floor; dimly lit sophisticated lamps hanging above oversized "VIP booths" creating a relaxing yet engaging ambience.

In the center of it all was the island-style bar. The display pulled the eyes in like a bug to a light; it was gorgeous. Soothing blue tones radiated from LED lights nestled just underneath the bar top. The bar top itself, upon second glance, appeared to be made of the same wood as the flooring and was apparently coated with some hard and sturdy epoxy or urethane finish. The barstools had four legs that caught an upside down pyramid seat made of black leather; very stylish. The center island was a series of coolers filled with various styles of beer, wine, garnishes, and mixers. The back bar, which was a giant display that sat on these coolers, was stocked appropriately with every high-end liquor you could imagine. Each bottle glistened in the hot white light projecting upward from underneath the translucent display racks. And to make this masterpiece stand out among everything else was an elegant waterfall, which had to be three feet wide and six feet tall, but it started on top of the coolers and seemed to actually go through the ceiling. It was the kind that trickled down a wall of rock; very appealing to the eyes. The waterfall was easily the first thing anyone sees when they enter this establishment, which in turn pulls people RIGHT towards the bar, which is exactly the effect it had on me. Genius. The whole setup was immaculate and I seemed to almost float towards it, setting my gaze to the Goliath waterfall and settling into one of the fancy pyramid barstools directly in front of it.

I was greeted almost immediately by the bartender, who casually tossed a bar napkin in front of me. "How's it goin', man?" he asked, and then flashed the pinky and thumb out hand gesture. He looked like he was in his mid-20's. He was clean shaven and had short, styled blond hair with half a tattoo sleeve on his left arm. He wore a black v-neck shirt and black dress pants. Based on his posture and smile alone, you could tell he was a ladies man. Maybe I should introduce my wife to him.

"I'll take a double whiskey and cola. Whatever you have for top shelf. Don't be shy." Like a monologue in a play that I had studied for ages, the words fell out of my mouth too easily. I missed this.

"You got it," the bartender said as he walked away. It was like he knew what I wanted, as he came back with a drink in his hand as quickly as he had walked away. He set the drink down in front of me.

"You wanna pay cash or start a tab?" he asked.

"Tab, please." He threw up his thumb and a curled forefinger, indicating he needed a credit card to hold to fulfill my request. I know how it goes; I'm no rookie.

"Hardly a nightclub," I noted as I looked around the bar, sending a blind hand to my back pocket to fish for my wallet.

"Nightclub's upstairs," the bartender clarified. "Hence the sign from the second floor that reads, 'Top Shelf Experience.' The nightclub upstairs is our 'Top Shelf Experience.' Get it?" He flashed that charming smile; he makes a decent living.

I nodded and met his smile with my own as I pulled a credit card from my now liberated wallet. He studied it briefly and looked back up with the same smile.

"Sounds good, man. Hey, if you need anything, my name's Cody." He held up his fist and delivered that thumb and pinky hand signal again, whatever that meant, and walked to the register.

"Thanks," I said passed a polite smile. I took a quick glance around the bar and considered the environment around me; not much else to it, apart from a few scattered customers throughout. I grabbed the glass of whiskey, folded and pinched the stirring straws to the side of the glass with my forefinger, met the glass to my lips, tilted my head back, and took a long slow pull as the ice teased and tingled my lips. It's charcoal goodness washed over my palate as I swirled it in my mouth over and over. The clouds parted, a choir sang in my head, my blood began to warm, and the hairs on the back of my neck began to stand on end; what a magic moment. I let out a breath of silent orgasmic air as the distilled spirits took over my body. I sat and stared at nothing as my mind took me back to my drinking days; trying to escape all of my problems, my family history of alcoholism, the colloquial drink at every family gathering. Then my mind shifted to when I finally quit drinking; the roses, the tree, the boom box, the note, my grandfather. Oh, my grandfather. The thought made my head spin, and then I suddenly found myself putting the whole drink down in a few gulps.

My eyes casually wandered the bar as I became more lost and intertwined by my thoughts. I was consumed by my past and memories of my Grandpa. I wasn't thinking about my failing marriage, though; I guess there's always a silver lining.

It's funny how he was kind of the reason for the beginning and the end of my drinking habits. I started to think about all of those memories and realized it was a bad idea; that road sign clearly says mental breakdown ahead. I shook the thoughts from my head as my eyes fell on something peculiar. On the final shake of my head, my eyes planted themselves on it. I had to stare pretty hard for a second to comprehend what I was seeing. It couldn't possibly be, but it was; the woman I had seen in my dream the other night. She was even glistening like she had in my dream. She was looking down at her phone, minding her own business; that same long black hair, the same exact evening dress. There was no way she was the same person, but then she looked at me. I could physically feel her gaze, and I knew.

"You," I whispered, and she pushed her stool back, got on her feet, and started out the door. "Hey! Dude! Guy! Cody!" I stumbled. Cody broke his conversation with the only couple left in the bar and shot a look in my direction.

"I need… could I get my…" I was fumbling over my words; my brain was thinking too fast for my mouth. "Fuck it." I tossed a twenty dollar bill onto the bar top and threw up a "thank you" hand. "Keep the change," I called out over my shoulder as I ran out the door towards the woman.

The rain was coming down hard now. When I didn't see her in the parking lot, I switched my glance between a few cars with no luck. I walked towards my car and I heard a car start to my left. My saunter quickly became a sprint as I saw headlights come from the same direction and heard tires begin to move over asphalt. By the time I got into my car, turned the key, flipped the headlights on, and threw it in gear, she was just pulling out of the lot and onto the road.

As if it was bad enough that my mind was on overdrive thinking of my wife cheating, the bullshit with the therapist, and the memories of my Grandpa that I had since repressed, now I've got to deal with wrapping my head around how a woman from my dreams was appearing in my reality? Was she some kind of witch? An entity? I threw my foot to the floor and caught up to her pretty quickly, but now what? She was doing about fifteen over the speed limit, but having caught up to her, I had nothing else to do but follow until she stopped at her destination. I could hear the trees whizzing passed me behind the sound of the downpour washing my car. I had felt guilty driving after I drank, in this weather, at this speed, but it was only one; I kept reassuring myself I'd be fine.

We were driving on a two-lane highway, and luckily there was no one else on the road. My concentration was broken by a familiar, but unknown, noise coming from inside the car; even though it was quiet, I made every extra effort to bring complete silence throughout the cabin to figure out what it was. I even went as far as holding my breath, more reflexively than consciously. Something like a slow pulsating, it stopped after a few "pulses." The car was silent for a moment, and then there it was again. I looked on the seat next to me. Nothing. When I heard the pulsing again, I looked at the floor on the passenger side, saw a faint outline of light and realized where it was coming from; the world had become so irrelevant, so foreign to me, I didn't even realize the sound of my vibrating phone.

Who could it be? My wife? I'm sure she's really concerned of my whereabouts. *But what if something happened to you?* The thought makes me lightheaded. With one hand on the wheel, I reached for my phone with the other. No luck. I tried again, my eyes barely clearing the horizon of the dashboard. Strike two. The second round of vibrating coming from my phone had stopped. I gave the road one more quick look before I made a longer reach and watched my hand to assure a win this time. Just as I grabbed it, it gave a quick double vibrate indicating whoever it was left me a voicemail. I turned my phone over in my hand to see it was my wife who had been calling me; seven times, apparently, and five voicemails to match.

I shook my head and then remembered I was driving. When I looked back over the dash and tried to see the road, my eyes were instead met by a tree, about twenty feet ahead of me. I tried to slam on my brakes, but they were useless. I heard a crunching sound for a split-second and then my world went black.

6

I pulled a huge gasp of air into my lungs like I had just finished holding my breath for a half hour. What's going on? What happened to me? I was sitting up in my bed, dripping sweat, heart racing, trying to piece together the incident that had just occurred. But I was in bed; with no injuries or bruises anywhere on my body that I can find. Was that a dream? Not possible; everything was far too vivid. Then explain getting out of that accident unscathed? Easy, I was positioned in the car in such a way that I wasn't flung in any direction or the car hit the tree just right and absorbed most of the shock of the crash. I guess there was only one way to find out.

I made my way downstairs, walked to the front of the house, and peered out the huge bay window to find my car parked in the driveway, untouched. But that was impossible; everything that just happened to me just… happened. The therapy session, the bar, her. Her. That woman. Was I losing my mind or did I see the physical embodiment of a woman I saw in my dreams at the bar I was taking a break from my life at? I had to be losing my mind; it's the only logical thing that explains my having been in an accident with no visible evidence that I had been in it. My best option at this point was to just pop a couple sleeping pills, make my way back up to my bed, and sleep the crazy off. And that was exactly what I did. Those sleeping pills shut my brain down and left me in a calm, subtle state; and I slowly began to drift. And before I knew it, I was fast asleep; and then I woke up on that island again.

I didn't wake up abruptly as I had last time, nor was I standing. I was laying on my stomach, resting on the sandy floor beneath me. I could hear the waves crashing all around me this time, which was relaxing; I didn't want to open my eyes or get up and venture around. Something, however, pulled my eyes open and brought me to my feet. I glanced around and confirmed my suspicions; this damn island again. It was identical to the way I had dreamed of it before; grayscale, desolate, depressing, calm. This dream was essentially a dead end.

I had nothing else to do but ponder my thoughts for the next… I have no idea how long this dream is going to last. Could be forever. I took in a deep breath, let out a sigh, threw my hands in my pockets and headed to the shoreline.

The environment was very relaxing; it put my mind at ease. I began to go over in my head the events of the recent past, but this time my brain wasn't some whirring machine overwhelming my entire thought process by racing through thoughts one after the other. This time I could sort through everything one by one, thinking of different details, aspects, breaking them down in my head, and actually digest what had been going on for a change; it was nice.

My thoughts started to falter, so I shifted them towards the events of last night; or tonight, rather. Seeing that woman at the bar was the strangest thing I'd ever experienced in my life. Was she real? Just a figment of my imagination? Was last night real? Looking at my car parked impeccably in my driveway proved otherwise. If she was real, how did she get there? How did she know I was there? And what was she doing there?

"Trying to get you home safely," a soft voice called from over my left shoulder. It caught me off guard; I whipped around so fast, I hadn't completely finished walking and I tripped over my own feet. My elbows caught me quietly in the sand, like I landed on feathers. After I made my impact, I looked up and there she was. That white dress; that black hair; that pale, shiny skin. She was unmistakable. We locked eyes as the waves crashed onto the shore behind me. Time stood still, frozen in my tense anxiety.

"You," I finally said, after I couldn't bear any more silence. "You. It was you," I kept repeating over and over, trying to make sense of everything. It was as if her appearance short-circuited my brain and nothing made sense anymore.

She sat patiently in silence, an incredibly somber smile decorated on her mouth. She looked very familiar, but I couldn't quite place my finger on it. She possessed many of the same qualities of someone else I knew. But who?

"You were the woman I saw at the bar," I managed to blurt out beyond my incessant rambling.

"I was," she replied calmly.

"And in my dreams… and… but how? How were you…? How did you…?" I couldn't finish any questions I had; I was so beside myself, I was at a loss for words.

"It's not important," she explained.

"Not important?!" my demeanor shifted from vulnerable and confused to angry and spiteful. "What do you mean not important?" I began to crawl back up to a stand. "I saw you in my dream a few weeks ago, on this exact… island, I guess." I threw my arms up all around me and quickly scanned this desolate state of solitude. "And then I head to some random bar that I've never even heard of to have a drink to find who there? That's right: you! So, I chase you in my car to get answers, crash into a tree, and wake up in my bed—bruise-less and cut-less, might I add—with no signs of ever having gone to the bar. No damage to my car. Nothing! But I definitely went there! I remember leaving the therapist's office and seeking out any bar I could find." I stood there for a few minutes remapping the entire scenario again, aloud this time. I was speaking to this woman, but I was more saying it to myself; for myself.

She continued to wait calmly for me to finish my rant, and she did nothing more than repeat herself. "It's not important."

Now I was enraged, I started to see red. "I want fucking answers!" I pointed to the ground like I was blaming the sand. "Are you some kind of fucking witch? Huh? Do you enjoy fucking with my head?! Answer me!" I took a step closer to her, my finger switching to her direction. "I want to know why you were at that bar! I want to know how you knew I'd be there! I want to know…"

"It's all so unimportant," she cut me off.

"It's fucking important because it doesn't make sense!" I could feel the rage taking me over. This is how I got when I drank; I was belligerent. Feisty. I had a short fuse and no one could fuck with me. I was at my wit's end. I took another step closer. Now my finger was right in her face and I could feel her breath brushing my nose. Or was that just my breath bouncing off hers and back onto me? It's not important.

"I got you safely home from a place you didn't need to be." Her eyes began to turn red and her smile slowly faded. "You know better. You know you know better. Everything else is unimportant."

I couldn't take her using that phrase anymore; I snapped. I'm not a fighter; I'm not a physical person. Even when I used to drink and burst out in a fit of rage, I wouldn't get physical; I just had a verbal temper. For some reason, this time, it was different. Maybe it was the comforting, nostalgic feeling of being inebriated again. Maybe it was the accident that apparently never happened. Maybe it was the fact that my wife cheated on me. Maybe it was a combination of everything, but everyone has their breaking point; and I had reached mine. I barely let her utter the last syllable of "unimportant" before I snapped both hands out like a viper to its prey. I latched onto her throat and squeezed like a constrictor. My outrageous episode was encumbered by her gaze, which turned into an unwavering, sinister grin, her eyes now red hot pokers. She wasn't even phased by me; it was like my rage empowered her.

"You fucking monster!" I shouted at the top of my lungs, and then I sprang up out of my bed. My hands were around my own neck and I was dripping sweat. I was back in my bedroom.

7

The human brain is a versatile, malleable tool. You'd be surprised the kind of abuse it can bear. It never failed to surprise me with what it could put up with in trying times. This was no exception.

I was fully conscious and aware as this night unraveled, which makes everything that happened that much more bizarre. I'll do my best to make sense of everything that transpired and explain it, but I couldn't that night, so I'm sure I'll be hard-pressed to try now. I was whisked away in a whirlwind from the island and was brought back to reality, or what I assumed was reality, and had no control over my body.

As I pounced forward in my bed with my fingers wrapped tightly around my esophagus, my heart pounding, I could feel my own grip growing stronger; there was nothing I could do about it. I relaxed my diaphragm and tried to pull some air into my lungs; no luck. I grimaced a few times and then tried again, striking out at every attempt. I started to get light-headed and fell back into my pillow. It must've been made of glass, as it made a crashing sound on impact and I fell into a hole of nothingness.

I fell for a short time before I landed on the floor of my boss's office, face first like I was getting ready to do a push-up.

I looked up in time to see my boss standing behind his desk with his arms outstretched, presenting his office to the detective who was standing opposite him. An intense look was shot from the barrel of the officer's face as my boss said, "I'm a businessman, Jack."

"And what are you in the business of, exactly?" responded the officer.

"That's my business," my boss said with a devious sneer.

I slowly brought myself up into a more comfortable position, resting half of my body on my left leg and the other half on my right foot.

"Do you think this is some kind of joke?" the officer painted a disgusting look on his face.

My boss's sneer remained. "A joke? Jack, I spent five years in prison for a crime that you can't prove I committed."

"You did it," the officer cut his speech off.

"It was never proven," my boss regained his place on his soapbox. "I graduated high school when I was 16 years old. I got a Master's Degree in Business Administration as well as a Bachelor's in Finance with a concentration in International Business. While I was in prison, I learned over 7 languages among countless other trades and skills that to most would seem futile, I found to be quite practical, actually."

"Bullshit," said the officer.

"It's amazing, the knowledge one's brain can absorb through speed reading and copious amounts of alone time." He said this in Chinese, which is odd that I understood him because I don't speak Chinese. Fucking dreams. He continued in English, his smile faded.

"I've been called a lot of things in my life; I've dealt with all of 'em. But I am not some fucking psychotic, makeup-wearing clown. So, no, I don't think this is 'some kind of joke.' Now, if you'll excuse me, I've got a business to run and unless you've got $10,000 you can fork over for the remainder of the hour, you can see yourself out." He straightened his tie and flashed an artificial smile. "Have a great fucking day!"

"We've got more questions for…"

My boss cut him off, "If you've got more questions, I suggest you write me a fucking letter." He stared hard at the officer for a few moments. "If you don't want to see yourself out, I can have you escorted out." He slowed down his repeated salutations sardonically. "Have. A. Great. Fucking. Day."

The officer accusingly pointed his finger at my boss. "This isn't over."

My boss scrunched his face, rolled his eyes, and threw a palm up in the air in a very "Who says that?" kind of gesture as the officer walked out the door.

I didn't get a chance to witness anything else that happened; I felt like I got punched in the stomach as some invisible force pulled my core to the wall and sucked me through it like a rag doll. I crashed into a seat that took the wind out of me. A very familiar voice echoed through the room and caught my attention: my own voice.

"There's a crucial component in life that we seem to forget about until it's staring us in the face; that inevitable reality is death…"

As I looked around the room, I began to make sense of the new world I was in; my grandfather's funeral. I was sitting two rows back in a pew at the church my grandpa went to every single Sunday since I was born. I remember presenting this eulogy like it was yesterday. My grandfather was the world to me. His passing was the death of me.

"No words can be said to bring the life we lost back to us even for a moment, but a formal goodbye can help us move on and bring peace to our souls." I was mouthing the words as I continued to take the church in, mournfully reminiscing the divine artwork between crosses, paintings, and stained glass scattered about the house of God.

My concentration was broken as my speech removed my grandfather's name and inserted my own. I reflexively turned my attention to the podium, where my wife was standing instead of me. My voice continued as normal with my wife mouthing the words as though she was the one giving the speech; my grandfather's name continued to be replaced by mine.

It was all confusing until I noticed the picture nestled in the easel beside the casket; it was me. This was my funeral. I gathered from the identical speech that I was dead by my grandfather's same murderer: cirrhosis of the liver.

The idea didn't sit well with me; my grandfather was a heavy drinker which lead to his ultimate demise. I was a heavy drinker; it's hereditary. His death shook me sober. I hadn't had a drop of booze since the day he died; I feared I'd reach the same eternal fate and leave behind someone who cared for me as much as I cared for him. My recent trip to the bar, whether it really happened or not, now left me feeling extremely guilty.

With everything that had been going on in my life, I failed to contain and maintain all of my core values and everything I believed in that represented me as a person. Regardless of whether this was a dream or a vision of a future that could be, it rattled me sober... yet again. I promised myself, in that moment, that I would take some time every day to remember myself and work on getting myself back to how I used to be before... all of this.

Just as I had internalized and digested all of this, I fell through the pew and began falling again. When I emerged on the "other side" I was winded yet again by my elbow as I landed on my side and rolled to the bottom of a small hill; it was another familiar landscape. I came to my hands and knees and began to shake the feeling of vertigo out of my head. I heard a faint whimpering sob not ten feet in front of me and that's when it hit me; a rush of emotions swept over me. My vigorous head shakes slowly dissolved into a slow, careful cadence as I began to sob.

I didn't look up. I didn't fucking need to; I knew EXACTLY where I was. And I knew EXACTLY who was crying. Those emotions made a second wave through my body; anger, frustration, happiness, disdain, every emotion I experienced on that day and every emotion in every experience that was a reflection of that day whisked in and out of me. They flushed around inside my head, taunting me and pulling me apart from the inside out.

I finally gathered the courage to look up. My head cautiously tilted upward and my eyes were met with the heavy scene. My vision was blurred through a mess of tears, but I knew exactly what I was looking at; a tattered, disheveled man, sitting on the ground with his back to a tree. His arms were tossed effortlessly on his knees and his head was slumped towards his lap. A bed of scattered roses decorated the grass around him and the sounds of "At Last" by Etta James coming from the boom box next to him was doing a nice job drowning the nearly inaudible weeps escaping that poor broken soul.

I eagerly awaited the next scene to play out, as I knew it would turn my mood around. I missed that feeling; that feeling of wanting her, getting her, and then wanting more.

I was robbed of the preceding moments as my body was turbulently wrenched from the scene yet again.

Everything in my imagination went black for a little while. It was so peaceful, so mellow, so gloomy, so eerie. I couldn't reflect on anything I had just experienced; all there was was the nothingness of my subconscious. When my body jolted back to life, my head jerked up and I looked around to make sense of my body's placement in the universe again. I realized I was laying completely flat face down with sand all over my face. I was on that island again; that sweet, beautiful, pitiful, mundane, somber island.

I noticed that woman was standing not five feet in front of me, patiently awaiting my arrival back from… hell? Did she send me through all those dreams? Did that rush of all of those emotions come from her forced will into my subconscious? Who the hell was this woman? What the hell was this woman? She must be a witch. There is no other explanation. At any rate, I was at her command. I was not worthy.

The film reel of things that have been, things that could be, things that are going to be, whatever it was that they WERE, played through my mind again, quickly this time, and in an abstract manner. No particular scene flashed in my head, but all of the emotions surged through all at once again. I began to cry uncontrollably. I scurried to my knees and crawled to her feet like a shameful peasant.

"I surrender! I surrender!" I cried out.

She flashed a smug half-grin that Mona Lisa would've been proud of.

"Stop being so dramatic," she said.

I sat in contemplation for awhile, consuming and accepting her words as I let my weeping dissolve into a whimper.

"Who are you?" I asked her feet.

"That's not important. What is important is that everything in your life is tangled. You are so consumed with your own thoughts that you can't even tell what's real apart from what's not anymore. You're tired. You're frazzled, tattered, at your wits end. I need to save you from your perilous fate before the proverbial straw that breaks your back takes you to a different place; a place where I can't exist. I can't have that."

How did she know all of this about me? What WAS she? I needed to just let die the never ending obsession to know things.

"What are you?" I finally met her eyes.

She seemed to ponder the question for awhile. "I am the answer to your unconscious cry for help. I am the beacon of light that's been flooding all of the dark corners of your life. I am the parameter necessary to make it right."

"To make what right?"

"Your life," she said.

"How do you know my life is… wrong?" I interrogated.

"I know more about you than you know about yourself. I know everything about you. I have for quite awhile. Every chance I can take to swim around your subconscious and learn what I can about you, I do. I can recall memories from your past that you've long since forgotten. It's in my nature."

"But how do you know all of this? How are you 'swimming around my subconscious'?" I couldn't wrap my head around what she was saying.

"Why is it necessary for you to wrap your head around what I'm saying?" It was like she was reading my mind. Apparently she could; apparently, she could do much more than that. She continued. "You need to learn to accept things for what they are instead of demanding to know the 'whys' and the 'hows' of everything that happens outside of your control. Sometimes you need to just let things…"

I looked up at her. "Let things what?" I asked.

She responded with a word that sounded like a blend between "be" and "see," either completing her statement, "Let things be," or turning my question into an example of what she just said to me. "See?"

I pondered the notion for a moment. I decided to just "let it be." "Do you have a name?"

"Sea," she said.

"Yeah, I'm passed that. What is your name?"

"My name is Sea," she said.

I paused. "Like the letter?"

"Like the word."

"Like the body of water?"

"Like the name. S-E-A. Sea. My name is Sea."

"Like the body of water," I repeated to myself.

"You don't always have to be right. I'm not named after water. My name is simply Sea."

"And sea is a body of water," I argued.

"For all you know, somebody could have just dreamt me up one day and decided that my name was going to be Sea. For all you know. Accept that my name is Sea and move on."

Her personality reminded me of someone, but I couldn't quite place my finger on it. And, considering the mental angst she'd put me through in the recent past, I found myself wildly attracted to her, oddly enough. She had absolutely gorgeous eyes, just like you had. It was as though I could see her soul when I looked into them. Between that and her personality, she put me at ease quite effortlessly.

I came back to her "purpose" for a moment. "To make my life right." Those words resonated with me because my life is so wrong. Life is so hard and nothing seems to make sense right now. Everything is coming unglued and I don't know how to put it back together again. And then she read my mind again.

"Sometimes, the world doesn't make sense; it just doesn't make sense. So many terrible, cruel things happen that we can't seem to wrap our minds around. That taxing, simple question repeats over and under in our minds: Why? Why? Why did it have to happen? Why did it have to happen to me? Why? While it may not be clear to you today, I can guarantee if you reflect on any disaster you've experienced in the past, you can link the chain of events that leads to something great that came out of it. Everything has its place in the universe. I promise you this much: Life can be hard. Life IS hard; but if you seek to find the silver lining, the world becomes a much less scary place. It may be hard to dance in the rain sometimes, but just look for the sunshine behind the clouds; rainbows are a symbolic reminder that even in the darkest of thunderstorms, something beautiful is waiting for us on the other side."

Those words weighed heavy in my mind. I had nothing else to do but absorb them, download them into my subconscious, and move on, returning to that monologue at a later date. After a long silence of consideration, I decided to change the subject.

"Do you know anything about this island, Sea?" I asked.

"This is the prison you've created for yourself in your own head," she explained. "It's so desolate and barren because this is what you've created for yourself. This is what you represent. It hasn't always been this way, though."

"How did it used to be?" so many questions, but my mind wasn't overflowing at all. I felt a sense of comfortable peace being in her presence; like I'd known her my whole life.

With that question, she stared at me hard, as if to say, "What did I just tell you about needing to know everything?"

I threw my hands up in a surrender and bowed my head slightly. "Ok, ok," I said with a charming half-smile. I pondered what to say next before I spoke up, choosing my words carefully along the way; I figured it was the smart choice, considering her challenges against my angst. "So, what do we do? Are you going to 'fix me'? How does this work?"

"You have problems controlling your anxiety and your aggression. As a result, you plummet yourself into a depressive state, which in turn makes you more anxious. This cycle is what's turned your marriage to turmoil."

I slumped my head in shameful defeat. "Yeah, I know. I can get out of control sometimes." I didn't know what else to say. I'd never really broken myself down and exposed myself to my problems; I usually just run away from them.

"You need to stop running away and actually confront your issues for a change." How is she doing that? I considered what she said and nodded cautiously to myself. "But that's not to say you're entirely at fault for the condition of your marriage." This caught my attention; my focus shifted and my head jerked up as my eyes met hers.

"How do you mean?" I asked.

"Communication is a two-way street," she said. I chewed on these words for awhile. Everything she said was so philosophical. It's like she exclusively spoke in code; a code, however, that I had no trouble cracking. It was so deep, but it all made sense to me.

"Communication is a two-way street," I repeated to myself. I thought of all of the issues I had been having in my marriage; I think ninety percent of them boiled down to this problem. Those five simple words lifted so much weight off of my shoulders. It was like I was trying to solve for x, and I had just been given the value for y. Now all I needed to do was finish the equation. I already felt better. Whoever this woman was, she was incredible.

"Can we talk about that?" I asked.

"Talk about what?"

"Communication being a two-way street. I want to talk about the issues I have with her and where that communication break comes in on both sides."

"Sure," she said, "Next time you fall asleep and we meet on this island."

My mouth opened, but before I had the chance to say anything, I opened my eyes and found myself staring at the ceiling of my bedroom.

8

I laid there for a bit while I realized where I was again. Once it made sense to me, I swung my legs over the side of the bed and rested my elbows on my knees. I buried my face in my open palms for awhile, painstakingly rubbing my eyes with my fingertips and then massaging my face with my palms.

Sea's words were my new obsession of choice. Surprise surprise. Particularly the part about communication; it's a two-way street. Communication is a two-way street. Well, this ought to be a fun counseling session today. I rubbed my face aggressively for a second while I turned some breath into a sigh and then stood up to begin my day.

I went through my clockwork routine to prep myself; go to the closet and pick out clothes, do a little grooming of myself before I hop in the shower, wash all body parts while I'm in the shower as necessary, get out, dry off, dress myself appropriately, throw on some after-shower essentials—deodorant, cologne, hair gel, the works—brush my teeth, and look in the mirror right before I head out to lie to myself that I'm a decent human being and it's going to be a good day. It's all rather typical; nothing to write home about.

I made my way downstairs to find my wife cooking breakfast. What? She hadn't done that in years. I scoffed in my head, but skipped the argument; I wasn't in the mood. I was in a surprisingly good mood after my encounter with Sea. Strange, this was probably the best mood I had been in since… in a long time.

My little JellyBean was smashing on some scrambled eggs while she danced away in her seat to some tune that must've been playing in her head. A smile was advertised across her face in big neon lights that said, "Come join me in my happiness." Such a sweet little girl.

"I made us breakfast," my wife said.

"I see that," I said with as much neutrality in my tone as I could muster. "But why…" She shot me a "not in front of our child" look, so I carried the "why" out for a moment into, "don't I fix myself a plate?" She looked down at the dishes she had already prepared with eggs, bacon, & toast and handed me one without looking back up at me.

"Well," I said matter-of-factly and sat down with my fully catered Breakfast-A-La-My-Wife. I started to construct an egg sandwich on autopilot as my brain went elsewhere. "Rainbows are a symbolic reminder that even in the darkest of thunderstorms, something beautiful is waiting for us on the other side." That's a rather profound statement; sounds like something I would've said back in my "glass is half full" days. I needed to get back to those days. Lately I've felt like life is just a series of events that didn't go the way you wanted them to and you're just supposed to find a way to go, "This is OK," and be convincing enough to believe yourself.

I mentally came back to my breakfast date for a moment to find my wife staring at me with an expression on her face like I was about to tell her what was in Area 51.

"What?" I asked innocently.

Her eyes darted back and forth a few times between mine before she squinted for a moment and opened her mouth like she was going to say something. When she either forgot what she was going to say or decided she didn't feel the need to say it, she shook her head in surrender and looked back at her plate. Her eyes widened even more as she took a deep breath, puffed her cheeks, and blew a sigh of hot air through her lips.

"What?" I asked again, more defensively this time. She continued her breakfast and threw up a very passive-aggressive hand and said, "Nothing," almost inaudibly through a mouthful of eggs and bacon. I carried my wrongfully accused expression from my wife to my daughter in hopes that maybe she could help me out with the communication break; no such luck.

I didn't bother wasting too much time trying to figure her out. Instead, I finished my breakfast, turned my plate into the sink, and relaxed, letting the day unfold as it would on my day off. With Sea on the brain, I knew most of my day would consist of me being in my own head, sorting out all of the info she laid out in front of me.

I checked my watch to gauge my place in the day. It was 10:30 AM on the 11th. I had plenty of time in the day to take a mid-morning nap. Something about the way I slept last night had me feeling well-rested but exhausted at the same time. It was as though I slept for too long and spent too much time dreaming in REM sleep.

On second glance, however, the date piqued my interest; August 11th. Why was that date so familiar? I had a feeling that was an important date that I shouldn't be forgetting.

And then it hit me. Shit. August 11th was my wedding anniversary with my wife. How could I ever forget that? I could think of a reason. I looked up from my watch to ensure my wife didn't notice my realization; I was safe. I had to think of an escape plan to pick up a card & flowers and I had to think of one quick. My day of relaxation quickly wilted away as I considered my options.

I left something at work? I was called in for a few hours? I had a meeting I forgot about? I was sleeping with my secretary? That last suggestion made me audibly laugh at its irony.

"What's so funny?" my wife asked as she surprised me from around the corner.

"Oh, I was just laughing at the irony of," I caught myself. "I left something at work."

"What was it?"

I started thinking on my toes. "Something for JellyBean," I said without hesitation.

"And what's ironic about that?" she wondered.

"Well, I left a note on my computer reminding me to grab it before I left," I explained.

"Yeah?" she dragged the word on in anticipation.

"I took the note off right before I left, but after I threw it in the trash, my boss came in and distracted me. So, I totally forgot to grab it before I walked out the door." I was good; I almost believed my own fib.

She gave me a very dissatisfied look and accompanied it with, "I guess I just don't see the irony."

"Anyway," I ignored, "I need to run in and grab it really quick. I'll be back in a few."

"I'll be here."

After considering the interaction again, I realized it was a poor lie; feeble, really. I didn't even tell her *what* I had gotten. She knew I was up to something, but I didn't care. It bought me time out of the house to be alone; oh yeah, and to buy an anniversary card for my wife.

I pulled into a parking spot at the pharmacy by my house, shut off my car, got out, locked it, threw my keys in my pocket and headed inside with some pep in my step.

I charged through the automatic doors and made a B line for the aisle marked "Greeting Cards/Gift Accessories." I found the section designated for Anniversaries and scanned my options. Did I want "Humor"? No, that seemed hardly appropriate. I didn't want too sappy and romantic either; I don't think we're really at a place in our relationship for that right now.

I tried finding one equipped with, "We made it this far, kiddo. I'll always love you, but I don't really like you right now." I quickly realized they don't make anniversary cards like that.

After getting my hands on a few and either laughing, cringing, or not even finishing some of them, I grabbed the one that seemed like a nice fit.

It was simple: it had an elegant assortment of watercolor flowers painted on the front with "Happy Anniversary" written in the upper right corner in a fancy font. When the reader opens the card, they're met with a short verse:

"On this day, years ago, our two souls became one in Matrimony.

Until this day, I have done all I can in my power to honor that union.

From this day, I promise to continue   to love, to honor, and to cherish, to keep our souls bound in the years to come."

It was still a little sappy, but it was simple and effective. I'm sure my wife will be pleased. I grabbed an envelope from behind the stack of cards on the shelf and slipped my card into its flap. On my way to the register, I walked passed the flowers; I forgot those, too, were on my agenda.

I stopped and looked for a bouquet that wasn't too over-the-top, but looked like I still tried. I found a nice bouquet mix of red roses and white daisies, accented with some baby's-breath and random greenery.

I reached in to grab the bouquet, but once I closed my grip and began to pick them up, I realized it was too much. With everything that was going on, I don't think my wife much deserved these flowers. Maybe once we get back to the way we used to be, *if* we get back to the way we used to be, I could go back to *my* old ways of romantically spoiling her. Besides, if I didn't get the flowers delivered as I usually do and I instead came home with a bouquet, it would be obvious why I went out. She would know I forgot about our anniversary. I don't need anything else to argue about.

I set the bouquet back down into its place and started toward the register again. Before I left the display of bouquets, my glance was met by a vase full of roses and a sign that read, "Single Stem Roses: $1.99." Why not? If I was looking to stay in the "simple yet effective" category, what better way to stick with the theme than a single stem rose?

I finally made it to the register with my card and rose. The cashier greeted me and we went through all of the formalities.

"Find everything ok?" he asked without looking up. Formalities.

"What? Yeah, thanks."

"Last minute anniversary shopping, eh?"

"How do you figure that?"

"You're buying an anniversary card with a single flower. You either forgot your anniversary or you hate your wife. Or both." He laughed at his assumption.

"You're good," I admitted.

"Both?" he asked with another laugh.

"Something like that," I said with a half-smile and a laugh so weak it barely made its way out of my nose.

The cashiers smile quickly faded and there was an awkward silence before he looked at his register and said, "$7.28, please."

He greeted a guest walking in as I went fishing for my wallet. I pulled it out of my pocket, opened its folds, and searched the pockets for my credit card.

I started in the pocket it belongs in; it wasn't there. I searched the rest of the pockets; no luck. I started to get a little frantic as I threw my hands into any pockets I could find in all of the articles of clothes I was wearing; still nothing. My anxiety piqued when I began to question the reality of the situation at the bar again. I ignored the feeling since I was in a rush and needed to get back home, so I came back to my wallet to stare at it for too long, hoping to find something that wasn't there.

I opened the fold of my wallet that housed my cash and lost myself in another trance. The twenty I didn't really use to pay my tab at the bar I never really went to was nestled safely inside. I tucked my tongue to the side of my mouth in a ponder and looked up at the cashier.

"Let me get this straight," I began out loud to myself. "I had a dream I went to a bar. I gave the bartender my card, which is now no longer in my wallet, even though it happened in a dream."

"What?" the cashier asked. He must've thought I was talking to him.

I ignored him and continued, really concentrating and trying to follow my thought process. "And even though it was a dream, I paid my bar tab with a twenty dollar bill, and said twenty dollar bill ended up back in my wallet, as though it was just a dream, but my credit card is missing like it wasn't a dream?"

The cashier stared at me hard with a really confused and uncomfortable face. When he was sure I was finished, he asked again, "What?"

I came back to reality and finally noticed the look he had been giving me during my monologue. I repeated his question back to him. "What?"

With nothing else to say, and not sure what else to do, he cautiously looked at the register, back at me, and then slowly said, "It's $7.28. Sir."

I handed the twenty over to the cashier. I didn't have time to sit around wondering why and how all of this weird shit was happening to me. The cashier popped his drawer, counted out my change, and handed it to me.

"Happy Anniversary," the cashier said to me as I walked away.

"You, too!" I hurried to the exit, stuffing the change in my pocket along with the receipt.

When I got to my car, I pulled a pen out of my center console, signed the card, sealed it in its envelope, and tossed the receipt in the back seat. I felt much better about my situation and consciously decided to not dwell on the fact that my card was missing from my wallet. My car was undamaged, I was undamaged, and the twenty was still in my wallet; all signs alluded to the fact that my trip to the bar was all a dream. It was as simple as that. Now stop thinking about it.

I pulled into the driveway of my domicile and straightened myself up when I got out of the car. It felt odd recognizing this occasion in this kind of scenario; it didn't feel genuine. At any rate, I walked to the door and straightened myself one more time before I walked in.

"Happy Anniv…" I started. I extended my arms out at the same time to present the rose and card to my wife, who was standing at the other end of the room, leaning on the wall with her arms crossed like she was waiting for me.

"What?" I said. Apparently this was my new mantra. Her response was a hard, piercing stare, but forgiving at the same time. She never looked down at what I was holding, she just kept gripping my eyes like they were the only thing holding her up against gravity.

Finally, she forced her weight against the wall to pull herself away from it. Her arms fell to her sides as she slowly sauntered towards me, not breaking her gaze. When she reached a close enough proximity, she gently placed her hands on the back of my head and pulled it down to hers.

I'm not sure if her intentions were to kiss me, but I assumed as much and forced her off of me with a push to her shoulders. I used a little more force than I had anticipated, which shocked us both. We had another moment of staring silence before I spoke up.

"I just… I don't think we're ready for that yet. *I'm* not ready for that yet. Sorry."

She continued to stare at me. When she finally looked at the contents of my hands, she snatched the card and the flower from my grip and stormed out of the room.

I focused on the archway after she was out of frame and took a moment to collect what just happened. How can she possibly be upset with me? I'm not the cause of all of this. And where was my credit card?

Knowing my wife wouldn't be bothering me for awhile, the day presented itself with the perfect opportunity for me to take my nap. And what better place for a nap than the family room couch; is that not where all naps are to be taken? With that thought, I sauntered over to it, kicked my shoes off, twisted my body around, and laid my body into its comfort. I tucked one arm up around and under my head as a makeshift pillow while I rested the other hand on my chest. I stared up at the ceiling briefly before I closed my eyes to drift away for a few.

I started to revisit the conversation between Sea and I: Communication is a two-way street. Rainbows are a symbolic reminder. Sometimes the world doesn't make sense. Everything she brought up repeated itself in an almost incomprehensible collage, weaving in and out of each other like a basket made exclusively of her wise words.

I felt something wet brushing my feet in a recurring periodic rhythm, first just the soles of my feet, but quickly advancing further to my ankles. When I finally made sense of what was going on, I opened my eyes and propped myself up on my hands; home sweet island.

9

I hadn't spent a lot of time perusing this island, wading the waters, relishing the breeze, but I had a feeling I'd be spending a lot of time here in the weeks to come; figuring out my life, my marriage, what lies ahead, and how my past affects me. Something about the island seems different this time. The grays, somehow, seemed more vibrant. I was no longer in a barren landscape; this island seemed more… homier.

Sea, of course, was waiting patiently for me. I pushed all of the questions stewing in my brain to the wayside. I just wanted to talk; I wanted to learn about her, I wanted to get more of her insight, and I wanted to hear about her past experiences that lead her to her deep philosophical nature.

I felt a deep sense of anxiety and a conflicting, unequivocal ease as I approached her. I don't know how one person, and I use that term loosely, could have such an effect on another, but I digress.

"Communication is a two-way street, huh?" I cast her way.

"What?" she asked honestly.

"What you said before. I…" I started, but my demeanor quickly shifted. "Where does it come from?"

"Where does what come from?" she asked. She continued to wear that amazing smile.

"Your insight. It has to come from somewhere. You don't just wake up one morning, have all of these deep ideas that really make you think logically, and jump into someone's mind and start playing around with the wires." I laughed at the thought.

"I don't know what to say," she admitted.

"There's a change of pace." There was some silence while I tried to think of where to take the conversation next. I couldn't ask her where she was from; that was irrelevant. She had to be local because she knew who I was. She obviously HAD to know who I was; how else would she have decided to get into my head? In that moment I realized I had made a conscious decision that she was a person that existed somewhere off of this island. What I hadn't decided was if she was here to fuck with me or here to help me. I was hoping it was the latter, but I was unsure after the stunt she pulled at the bar.

"What happened at the bar?" I quickly realized I'd get nowhere with that question given her last response to the same question, so before she had a chance to answer, I followed up with, "Why me?"

"Do you know what I love about nature?" she completely ignored both questions, but I still allowed her to pull the reigns.

"What's that?"

"If you study quantum physics, you learn that there's so much beautiful symmetry and chaos that exists in the same space within fractions of fractions of seconds."

"Yeah," this sounded all too familiar, but from where?

"But if you study astronomy, you find that the same can be said, but on a much grander scale. And while things happen within such a small time frame, there is more so that take millions upon millions of years to come to fruition. It's just astounding to me that such beauty can exist in spaces smaller than we can fathom while the same beauty can exist in such colossal spaces that we can't wrap our heads around it. That's beauty in its purest form."

She was beauty in its purest form, but she had a point. And "colossal" was the trigger word that reminded me where it came from. I must've gotten so lost in my work, and I'm sure as a result, lost from my relationship, that I forgot my old passions and hobbies. Both quantum physics and astronomy used to be my forte. And that monologue, EXACTLY what she said to the letter, is how I sold my passion to people. But how did she know that? This meeting was loaded with epiphanies as I realized further that finding out how she was doing what she was doing was just wasted breath. I was better off just playing her games, letting her pull the reigns, and enjoying the ride.

"So, what does that have to do with me?" I tried to word it appropriately to get SOMETHING out of her.

"Nothing!" she exclaimed with that smile.

"No," I carried the word on. "There's a reason you said that. You didn't just bring it up."

"What makes nature so beautiful?" she asked.

"You literally just said what makes nature beautiful; right back there when you explained quantum physics and astronomy."

"No, in its simplest form, what makes nature so beautiful?"

I really considered the question this time. After a long pause, she answered her own question.

"Because it's untouched by the human hand. It just… IS beautiful. It's beautiful on it's own. No matter what happens, it will always be beautiful."

I didn't get where she was going with this.

"You don't know where I'm going with this," she said to herself. I accepted, for a brief moment, that she knew how to read my mind. "Sometimes, whether we put our hands into it or not, things will be beautiful, or they will be chaos. Our influence bears no weight."

I crossed my arms and pondered that. For a long time. Whoever she was, this woman was incredible. I knew the answer to my next question, but I was curious how she'd respond. "So, what does that have to do with me?"

"You know the answer to that question."

"God dammit, you're good." I threw my arms to my sides. I didn't know how to take her; didn't know how to digest her words. And for some reason, I loved it.

"So, what am I supposed to do with that?"

"Take it," she said, "chew on it for awhile. Make sense of it. Apply it to your own life."

"Sounds simple enough."

"You have no idea. Now, think about it. You're waking up now."

"What?" I asked in a panic. The question hardly rolled off my tongue before I found myself drooling on my shirt on the couch. I was a little perturbed, to say the least. I wanted to get to know this woman. I felt a connection with this woman that I hadn't felt before, but I suppose epiphany number three would be the fact that I'll probably never get the chance to get to know this girl on a personal level. Whoever she was, she was here to coach me and give me sound, however deeply ambiguous and philosophical, advice, and I suppose my role in all of this is to just say, "Yes, ma'am, no, ma'am," take her advice, run with it, and try to better myself.

10

My midday nap left me feeling rather fatigued, but while it sounded exceptionally pleasing to close my eyes again and continue my slumber, a glance at my watch told me I spent too much time on the island to justify sleeping any longer. I forced myself off of the couch and went through my mental list of priorities I needed to take care of.

I went scrolling through typical household chores, but my mind kept going back to the credit card at the bar. In the off chance it wasn't a dream, my card would still be there, and I needed it, so it only made sense to go get it. And it wasn't a perilous feat: run in, run out, get on with my life. I had plenty of time.

My wife was probably still pouting upstairs, so I threw my shoes on and snuck out the door to my car. The day had become foggy by now, which matched my disposition. I was so tired, it was a wonder I even made it to the bar without falling asleep at the wheel.

I made it to Via734 in no time and pulled into a parking spot. I sat in my car and collected myself for a moment. I gently closed my eyes and gave them a few scrubs with the sides of my index fingers. My mouth popped as I reflexively took a breath to let out a yawn. Plan B: I'm getting this credit card, going back home, and crawling my ass into bed. That is, if I make it without falling asleep along the way.

I sauntered to the front door and made my way inside. By my luck, Cody was there again so I walked to the bar and stood right in front of him. He looked up at I placed my hands on the bar top.

"Hey, man," I said comfortably.

"Hey," he said, sounding confused. He was pulling dishes out of the dishwasher and stopped when I approached him.

"Just here for my credit card," I said matter-of-factly.

He stared at me for a second. "What credit card?" he asked, still confused.

"The credit card I left here. Remember? The other night. I came in, had a drink, paid with a twenty, and then left abruptly?" My story was choppy and my inflection suggested a question with every segment.

Cody's head began to swivel back and forth slowly while he said, "Dude, I have no idea what you're talking about." I stared at him blankly. "I've never met you before in my life," he continued.

"There's no way... There's gotta be," I had trouble finding the right thing to say while I pulled my wallet out. I opened the folds and checked the slot where my credit card belonged; there it was, nestled safely as though no one had ever tampered with it.

I didn't know what to say; I was beside myself. Before I had enough time to comprehend the gravity of the situation he said, "Maybe you're dreaming."

His words almost didn't make sense to me. "What?" I asked under my breath.

"Wake up," he said in Sea's voice.

In that instant, my head jolted forward and I darted my head around my car, taking in my new surroundings. Was I just dreaming? God, I really did fall asleep at the wheel; luckily I was already parked by the time it happened. I still felt pretty groggy even after my second cat nap, but I made it to the bar safely, so there's that.

In the typical "woke up on the wrong side of the bed" fashion, I was pretty annoyed with... really nothing at all, so I charged in through the front doors with conviction and walked straight to the bar. Cody was working in real life this time, or was it real life this time?

"Hey, what's goin on, man?" he asked as he, again, threw up his pinky and thumb to greet me.

"Hey, Cody, I'm just here to pick up my credit card that I left here the other night."

He made a concerned look before he debriefed me. "Your wife came and picked it up already. She didn't tell you she grabbed it?"

I was stunned. That was impossible; she had no idea I had even come here. "Are you sure it was my wife? She had no idea I came here. Did you check her ID?"

"Well, she knew you by first and last name and knew you left your card here. I guess I never thought to check her ID if she had all of that info." He thought about it for a second. "If it wasn't your wife, you've got yourself a stalker, bro." He flashed a playful smile at me with a kind of, lucky you, undertone to it.

"No, that's impossible. What did she look like?" I had an idea who the "stalker" was and I feared the answer to my own question, but I needed to know.

"I don't know, man. Skinny; pale; long, black hair; about 5'5". She had blue eyes."

Just what I thought; it was Sea. I was at a loss for words. I was losing my mind. She really *was* my stalker. How was she doing all of this? I was so beside myself I just stared at Cody, lost in my thoughts.

"Dude? Man? Bro…" he said, finally breaking my concentration.

"Yeah. Thanks. Ok. Thanks." I turned around slowly, shock still decorated on my face. I sauntered out of the bar as I fished my keys out of my pocket. I started my car and stewed in my confusion.

I had so many questions running through my head, I figured it would be best to shut it all away and talk to Sea at our next rendezvous. I laid my head on the rest, closed my eyes, and contemplated everything. A feeling of helplessness began to wash over me; I was so lost.

Every quest to find answers just lead me to even more questions. My affection towards Sea seemed to be unrelentlessly growing, while at the same time being challenged against the perception that she was single-handedly ruining my life; from the deep breeze of my mind working outward.

My initial temporary resolution was to just see my counseling sessions with my wife through and put up with Sea haunting my dreams, and apparently my reality, in the meantime. That burden felt too heavy to bear.

My inner conjunction of thoughts was interrupted by an undiminishing feeling that someone was watching me. I feared opening my eyes and finding out it was true. But something forced my eyes open, I'm assuming the reigns of Sea were hard at work again, and I slowly swiveled my head to meet the eyes of my stalker right outside my door.

We stared hard at each other for almost an eternity, the cars on the road behind her moving slower and slower until they reached an eerie pause. The world was still and the silence was deafening.

As clear as if she had been inside the car with me, she said, "You're home," quietly, but startlingly, as she slapped the palms of her hands onto my window. I shot up out of bed in a crippling panic, sweating pouring into my brows off of my forehead.

11

Oh, how I longed for a drink. My brain was so wound up that the only thing capable of untangling it was some hard liquor. I was so lost; I had no idea what the hell was going on. Two surreal dreams later, I surrendered the idea that I ever went to the bar and consciously cast out the conundrum of what the hell happened to my credit card.

"Let's try doing some role play, then, shall we?" My therapist's voice shook me from my trance. Lost inside my own head again; dammit, I really need to stop doing that. I stared at the therapist blankly.

"What?" he asked innocently.

"What?" I repeated back to him. His original question was a jumbled mess to me.

"I said let's do some role playing; role reversal. You play the part of your wife, and she plays the part of you. Is that something you feel comfortable doing?" Why was he being so nice all of a sudden?

"I suppose," I said unconvincingly.

"Actually," the therapist corrected himself, "Strike that. What I'd like to do today is try a little spin on role playing."

"How do you mean?" I asked cautiously.

"Well, you two are going to be interviewing each other."

"Like, for a job?" I questioned.

"No, just to be with one another."

"I don't understand."

"I'm going to have you each take turns asking the other anything you'd like to know: about yourselves, about the other person..."

"Doesn't sound much like role playing to me," I interrupted.

He stared at me hard for a moment. "Humor me," he said. My eyes widened in surrender. "Who wants to go first?"

"I'll go," my wife raised her hand in anticipation, a half smile shone across her face. She was really on board with this interview idea.

"Great!" the therapist responded. He looked at me, "So, she'll ask you a question, you just answer truthfully, and reciprocate a question to her. Sound fair?" I nodded. After accepting approval of my comprehension, he looked back at my wife, nodded in her direction, and said, "Go ahead." He leaned forward and placed his elbows on his knees. His hands came together with all of his fingers interlocking except for his index fingers, which stayed pointing straight up as his lips rested against them. He casually changed his attention between us as we talked, focusing hard on whoever was talking at the time.

My wife turned her chair so we were face-to-face, straightened herself in it, cleared her throat gently, and lifted her head to make eye contact with me. We stared at each other for what seemed like an eternity while I waited for the words to leave her mouth. I had a lot of emotions going through me again and I started to well up. A warm smile started to stretch across my wife's face until she saw my eyes getting wet, then it quickly transformed into a look of solace and concern. I shook my head subtly and she cleared her throat again.

"Who or what do you model your idea of love after?" she asked softly. What was she doing? She knew the answer to this question; we had discussed it before. She knows it's a sore subject for me, but I signed up for this, so I obliged. I cocked my head to the side and slowly nodded my head, forcing a grimace out of my mouth to let her know I knew what she was doing.

"Ok. You want to do this? Ok." My eyes moistened themselves again. "My father met my mother when she had brain cancer. All of her doctors were confident they'd be able to get rid of it. In the meantime, she had gotten pregnant with me.   When I was five, she became terminal, so they decided to get married. He did absolutely everything for her. He took care of her like her body was his own. It was as though they were one entity; like when they had gotten married, their two souls meshed into one being. He would bathe her. Every day. He would brush her hair afterwards. Every day. If she wanted to feel pretty that day, he would help her do her makeup. He cooked every single meal and ate together with her, and me, of course, every day, for months until she lost her fight against the cancer. Everyone asked why he'd marry her if he knew she was going to die soon. He said, 'It's not how long you love someone that counts. It's how much you can love them while they're still around. Whether it's a day or a lifetime, it's never enough time. But you should never let tragedy destroy you.'" With that last sentence I looked down and wiped a tear from my eye.

After watching what my father did for my mother, all of the steps he took to ensure that she was always as comfortable as she could be, I made a promise to myself that whoever I ended up with would be treated the exact same way he treated her. Any time someone asked me about true love, I ALWAYS went back to the relationship my parents had. There was nothing else to say at that point, but let the silence sort out the emotions billowing around the room.

Our therapist was staring passed us at nothing really at all, his position not moved from when she originally asked the question, just absorbing everything I had said. My wife was staring at me, that look of solace still fixed to her face. It was so quiet in the room, I could hear the seconds ticking away from the clock on the wall behind the therapist. I finally realized it was my turn to ask a question and spoke up.

"Um," I started, my voice booming through the room in an almost echo, "my turn?"

Without shifting his focus, the therapist nodded his head slowly as if he was in a trance.

I didn't waste any time exonerating the question that had been locked in my mind for quite some time by this point. "Do you trust me?"

"What?" she asked me like she knew that was the question I going to ask.

I enunciated the question more clearly. "Do. You. Trust. Me."

She folded her hands nervously in her lap and then searched them over for the correct answer. After she realized it was nowhere to be found, she decided to talk to them instead. "I mean, I trust you, but…"

"But what?" I became frantic for a moment as I cut her off. My therapist shot me a look in my anticipation and threw a "stop sign" hand up and a concerned look in my direction to calm me down.

With that, she looked at me, defeated.

"You're in your fucking head so much." This was huge. My wife never swore, unless she was radiating some major emotion, whether positive or negative. I unfortunately feared it was the latter in this situation.

"What do you mean?" I said reflexively. I new EXACTLY what she meant. I've done it my whole life. I live my life in my own head. The world happens and I rescind myself to the confines and comfort of my own space in my head and sort everything out. The world only makes sense to me when it's been processed and sorted in my own time away from outside influence. And I didn't know how to tackle her response.

She took a deep breath and tried to help me make sense of what she said, spilling choppy fragments of sentences along the way. "You… say things with relevance and then… you just… you pull yourself into this… like, different thing. It's hard to explain, it's like you're on autopilot. It's like you're there, but you're not there…" She continued for a moment, twisting and rolling her hands around each other in an attempt to get her point across. She wasn't making sense, but I knew exactly what she was talking about.

"If it's a problem for you, why haven't you brought it up to me before?" I asked.

"I have. Multiple times. You just look at me with that blank stare and nod obediently like you've been hypnotized." I didn't know what to say. I was floored. It all started to make sense to me. Like I said, I knew I did that, it was the only way I could make the world make sense to me. But just now, just in this moment, I had realized where the communication break had come from. "Communication is a two-way street." Sea wasn't defending my position, she was trying to tell me that I was the one who hasn't been communicating. I thought of all of the occasions where I had assumed my wife had trailed off in her rants because I just stopped listening. She wasn't shutting me out; just the opposite! I was shutting her out and going into my own head!

And then I reflected on how I thought she was suffocating me. She wasn't suffocating me; that was just more bullshit I fabricated in my head to sabotage my marriage. She didn't ruin this marriage by cheating on me; I ruined this marriage by being the anxiety-riddled monster that I am. I drove her to do the things that she did. She was never suffocating me; I was shutting down and worrying her about my own damn health! I think I'm going to be sick.

Tidal waves of guilt and remorse started to flood my brain. This session didn't go the way I had expected it to. At all. I didn't know what to expect, but I sure as hell didn't expect this!

"Hello?" my wife tried to snap me out of another episode.

"What?" I asked as I came back to the room.

"Do you love me?" she asked like she already had about ten times; she probably HAD asked me ten times. I need to learn to get in my head exclusively when I'm alone.

I stared at her trying to figure why she would ask me that. "Of course! Babe, after all we've been through, I will always love you. We may have gone down a bumpy road, but we always see it through. I can't believe you'd even ask me that."

"Well..." she looked back down at her hands. She shot a surprised look at the therapist and asked, "Can I ask him another question?"

"If it's alright with him," he gestured toward me. I have a name. That bothered me more than it should have. At any rate, I cocked my head to the side and nodded in forced agreement.

"Tell me the three most important things to you and why."

I placed the palms of my hands on my face and let my head fall backwards. That was such a loaded question and I really wasn't prepared to answer. My anxiety was through the roof.

"JellyBean is my number one; no questions asked. You know why," my therapist stopped me with his hand again.

"Assume she doesn't know you. Tell her who JellyBean is and why she's so important to you." I tried to kill him with my stare but failed, so I switched my focus back to my wife.

"Jellybean is my daughter. She's the best thing that ever happened to me. Her real name is Regina Bella. We always called her GinaBella, until I stumbled over my tongue one day and 'JellaBella' came out. From that point on, JellyBean just kind of stuck. She changed my life four years ago. Four years ago in exactly fifteen days, actually. I live for that little girl. I would die for that little girl. I sometimes wonder if my wife feels the same way." I paused to let my words sink into my wife's head. She deflated a little at the last sentence. I think she gets it. I continued calmly.

"Number two would have to be the memories of my grandfather. Since my father left when my mother died, he raised me ever since. I will always hold my memories of him dear to my heart. I was crushed when I found out he died. A part of ME died that day." I paused again when I noticed the therapist looked like he was going to say something. I raised my eyebrows to invite his question in.

"You said your father left when your mother died?"

"Yes. He lost his mind and moved to England or something like that. Just went nuts, I guess. Was never right again."

"But that's who you model your love after?"

"Yes."

"But he abandoned you at such a young age."

"Right." I pondered his line of questioning for a second. "I guess he just eventually let tragedy destroy him."

The therapist tried to mask his sympathy with a smile, but I saw right through it.

"I guess I didn't think of it," I continued. "I saw how much he loved my mom while she was around and that was a beautiful thing. Maybe I didn't forgive him when he left, but I accepted his abandonment. Besides, my grandpa probably raised me better than he ever could have. I still have an utmost respect for his love for my mom. I'll never forget that, and I'll do my best to be that way myself."

I don't know if he tried to trap me, or if I just trapped myself, but I regretted saying that last part in front of my wife. With the way things were going, regardless of this session, that's the last thing I wanted her to hear right now.

"What's the last?" my wife asked.

"What?" my focus turned back to her.

"What's the last important thing to you?"

I stared at her hard, shifting my focus from one eye to the other, and carefully considered her question. My words came out of my mouth sounding like a dagger looking to pierce her heart, but it wasn't my intention.

"My wife," I said with contention. The tension between us began to grow so thick, you could see it.

After another long pause my wife spoke up without breaking eye contact. "Why?"

Considering the contents of our discussion, feelings of love and understanding seemed to be misplaced. Only malcontent and resentment apparently filled the air. We stared at each other for an eternity. "I don't know," I finally admitted.

"What bothers you about me?" she wasted no time asking me.

I tried saying, "My turn," but I was cut off by her repetition of the question.

I leaned forward, placed an elbow on one knee, and placed the palm of my hand on the other. "I can't trust you," I said matter-of-factly.

My wife looked back to her hands for comfort, slowly nodded to them, and began to cry.

"I can't trust you. And it's beyond the fact that you fucked someone in our bed," she cringed at the curse word. "It's the little shit that bugs me even more. It's like, if I can't even trust you to not smoke, what the fuck CAN I trust you with? Can I trust you with my daughter?"

"Our daughter," my wife cut me off again. You could tell she was getting agitated. "And I am not smoking, where did you even come up with that notion?"

I could feel my blood pressure rising. What had seemed to become a slow progression towards a possibly healing marriage started to crumble back into the pile of rubble it had recently become.

"The night I was sleepwalking and almost ended up walking into traffic? Before I went back to bed, I poked my head out to see what you were up to, because I smelled cigarette smoke and I knew it could only mean one thing and lo & behold!" I threw my recently rested hand up in the air.

"I thought you were never drinking again…?" my wife asked under her breath.

My grimace fell off of my face immediately. "What?" I asked innocently.

"You said, you promised," she corrected herself, "that after your Grandpa died, you'd never touch another drink again."

"What's your point?"

"Explain the other night when you left here and went to the bar. I knew exactly where you were. And you can't trust me? You can't trust yourself!"

I sank back into my chair and let her words repeat in my head. "I never went to the bar," I said to myself, but loud enough that my wife thought I was talking to her.

"Yes you did. I know you did because… because I just know." My wife was sobbing uncontrollably now. "I can't have a simple fucking cigarette, but you can go and do that shit? Fucking bullshit!" She buried her face in her hands and fell forward, resting her knees on her elbows.

"I never went to the bar," I kept repeating to myself to try and make it true, "I never went to the bar."

I never went to the bar.

12

Breakfast: Arguably the most important meal of the day. At the least, it's my favorite meal of the day. Nothing beats a couple of eggs, scrambled or over medium, depending on my mood; hashbrowns, extra crispy; bacon; wheat toast; and a glass of fresh orange juice, pulp free of course.

For this particular occasion, I went over medium with my eggs and threw them onto my toast to make a sandwich which I was halfway through by this point. Puddles of yellow decorated my plate as I tore into it and watched the yolk bleed out over my toast and off my hands; fried eggs are always messy. My glass of orange juice was half full (hey, look at that) and there was a puddle of grease where the bacon used to be. The hashbrowns were untouched on account of my tradition of saving those for last; I don't know why I do that, but I always have.

It's been five days since my therapy session with my wife and a whole new host of questions were clouding my mind, the most prominent being how the hell she knew I went to the bar. I've been waiting patiently to pop up on that island and talk to Sea about what the hell's going on, but to no avail. In fact, I hadn't even dreamed about that island since the therapy session. No dreams at all, really.

Well, that's not entirely true. I had a couple arbitrary third person cinematic type dreams. One was about some nut job who broke out of a psych ward and terrorized the city. Another was about the end of the world and some "new" evolved species of humans. Nothing really crazy by dream standards.

I'd never gone this long without seeing Sea or being on the island since I've started dreaming about either one. If I was being honest with myself, I'd say I'm starting to miss her. In the same breath, considering I don't really know *what* she was in the first place, it's hard to say *what* I miss. I can't really place my finger on what it is I enjoyed about her; her presence made me comfortable and put me at ease, to put it bluntly. There were no particular aspects or characteristics of her that drew me to her; just her as a whole… person? Ghost? Subconscious? It was hard to say anymore. It had been so long since I had seen her, I hardly remember her even existing. It's like I dreamt the whole thing up! The irony made me chuckle to myself.

After careful speculation, I confided in myself that she was just a figment of my imagination and I resolved that I was just talking to myself. I accepted that. I guess the next step was working on my marriage.

I grabbed my napkin and brushed it over my mouth, cleaning off the traces of masticated food and grease that had collected around my lips. I rested my palms from outstretched arms onto the table and absorbed my surroundings. The pancake house was desolate at this time of day, only a few select patrons populated the tables.

It was lunchtime at work, so I decided to eat out today, and breakfast seemed like a good idea since all I had in the morning was my ritual cup of coffee. I sat alone in my booth and took the opportunity to reflect. I needed to be getting back to work, so I flagged down the server, requested my bill, proceeded to pay, and made for my car.

The rest of the day went smoothly, and before I knew it, I was walking in the front door of my house to find my wife on the couch with a book.

"What are you reading?" I asked sincerely.

"It's called *183 Ways to be Happy* by some guy named Shigs," she explained.

"What's it about?"

"It's not about anything, really. It's just a bunch of quotes he created from his own social media and then he tells an anecdote or gives an explanation of the quote. It's interesting, but it's kind of dry." Sounds like something I'd be interested in.

"Why's it called *183 Ways to be Happy*?" I pondered out loud.

"He has 183 quotes in total. I don't know about the happy part, though; some quotes are about being happy, some are about love, some are about sadness, about life. It's all really inciteful and philosophical. It really makes you think."

"Who's it by again?"

"Shigs?" she sounded unsure of the name. "I read about him online. He's actually a bartender at that Via734."

Ugh, don't remind me, I thought to myself. "What's a bartender doing writing a book?" I said aloud. "That's kind of strange."

"Yeah, I don't know," she replied. "I guess everyone has a hobby. He's written a few books, apparently."

"Must not be a very good author if he's still working as a bartender."

"To each their own, I guess. Some people don't take life seriously. It's all pirates versus ninjas to them."

Whatever that meant. After that almost too normal interaction with my wife, I took my shoes off, put my belongings away and sat down for dinner. The rest of the evening unfolded as normal. I finished dinner with my wife and JellyBean, took a shower, and turned in for the night.

The late hours of day were creeping up on me as I laid my weary head to rest. The only sound in the room was that of the box fan in the corner of my room that I kept on specifically for background noise. While we weren't cuddling, my wife and I slept in the same bed for the first time since she cheated on me; such a huge step for me. The moment my eyes closed, however, I was slipped back into a whirlwind of anxiety-driven questions. I didn't want to do this right now. But, alas, my brain didn't care.

No matter how hard I tried, my mind continued alluding to the fact that I had such a burning unanswered question for Sea that NEEDED to be answered. My trip to the bar cycled through my head repeatedly along with my wife's confession of knowing I was there.

Regardless, I was itching to talk to someone or some*thing* that didn't exist; never *did* exist, apparently. It's pretty wild what the mind will do to you under extreme stress. At any rate, I found it hard to shake the feelings I developed, real or not. It's been hard to find that lately. Oh well. Whatever. Nevermind.

I fell asleep before I realized it was even happening. The relaxing echoes coming from my fan slowly transformed into the lush sounds of waves crashing onto the shore. This awkward sense of subjugation fell over my body, and only then did I know I was in fact at the perils of my dreamscape. I opened my eyes and looked around. I was surrounded by the desolate landscape of this island again.

14

I knew what was happening and I wasn't prepared for it. I was sitting up on my hands with my legs outstretched on the sand. I just appreciated what my dreams had to offer me this time. I reabsorbed my self-fabricated island for a few and then rolled onto one side and got myself to my feet. Once I situated myself, I threw my hands in my pockets and started towards the shoreline.

The island was still very grey, and very solitary, and very depressing. I sauntered to the water with all the time in the world. I wasn't looking forward to talking to Sea, but I feared she'd be showing up whether I liked it or not.

But Sea was just a figment of my imagination, right? I had no reason to fear her presence. She wouldn't be showing up at all; it's just happenstance that I'm situated on this island yet again. I didn't need to talk to her anymore anyway; everything in my real life was slowly starting to get better.

I looked out onto the horizon to reflect on the turn around my life had made and the positive direction it was starting to go. Yeah, my wife and I had a lot of work ahead of us, but we were a work in progress. I didn't know if we were gonna work out or not, but I definitely felt better about the marriage than I had a few short weeks ago. Who knows? Maybe someday in the future I could get passed what she did to me.

The sky reflecting off the water made a field full of dancing diamonds on the grey oasis that seemed to stretch on forever. The sound of the crashing waves onto the shore tickled my eardrums and filled my body with a sense of comfort and tranquility. I stopped walking, sat down in the sand, hugged my knees, and appreciated the serenity of the scene.

Some time went by before I felt the presence of somebody behind me and I knew whose weight it was that I felt. I guess she wasn't a part of my imagination after all. Or maybe she was. Or maybe some part of my subconscious—her— decided to make its way back into my reality, or sub-reality I suppose. "I have a bone to pick with you," I acknowledged calmly without looking back.

She let a few more waves crash before she replied. "You're angry." I couldn't tell if she was telling me or asking me.

"Perturbed," I corrected her.

"There are no words I can say that would change your emotions or the way you express them," she said.

"Then I'll just speak," I started calmly. "I haven't known you for very long." I laughed. "Listen to me; I say that like you're real. Fuck, I guess you could be real. I really don't know anymore. I don't know what's real or what's fake. I don't know what's right and what's wrong. Hell, I don't even really know whether I'm dreaming or not anymore." I paused and gave her a chance to reply. She obviously didn't have anything to say, so I continued, still focusing on the horizon in front of me.

"Before I conjured you up in my mind—or when you broke your way into my mind by some weird voodoo magic shit, that I still don't know—I hated my wife; just fuckin' hated her." I considered my last statement. "Correction: I've always loved my wife with everything in me. My soul skipped a beat the moment I met her; I felt an energy surging inside of me that I'd never felt before we first locked eyes. When she… it makes me sick to even think about it. When that happened, my world came undone. I was so lost, I didn't even know what to do with myself. My soul was so crushed, I even considered…"

"I know," she interrupted me. "I had to interject and shift your focus to keep your mind off of it."

I considered what she said. What was she talking about? Interject and shift my focus? And then it hit me: when I was thinking about killing myself at my desk in my office and I heard a lady's voice call out, "No."

I swiveled my body to face her and rested a leg on the sand. She was sitting sideways on her right leg, resting her weight on the same side arm while playing with a patch of long grass with the opposite hand. "That was you?" I shot her an accusatory look. "That was you that said, 'No,' to me in my office that day."

She flashed her Mona Lisa smile and said, "Sorry to interrupt. Please, continue your soap box monologue."

I laughed at the sarcasm and then immediately realized my original frustrations and resumed my accusations.

"No," I shook my head, "That was you in the office that day; or, in my head, or whatever. You somehow pushed me to safety from oncoming traffic while I was sleepwalking. You helped me see things about my relationship that my therapist couldn't even bring to light. But you," I looked at the sand and thought about my next conviction critically. I met her eyes again and continued very carefully, "You were at that bar. You left abruptly when I noticed you. I followed you on the road and crashed into a tree, but when I woke up, my car was untouched. I was untouched!"

Sea shook her head, her smile unfaded. "You went to the bar that night. You never saw me there. You finished your one drink and were so exhausted and distraught that you didn't even realize you had fallen asleep. You began sleepwalking, so I coaxed you into safety. I lead you out of the bar in your dreamscape. Your wife actually was trying to call you when you thought she was, but you never hit a tree; you just blacked out. Interestingly, you're an incredible sleep driver."

"Oh, bullshit!" I interrupted. "You're lying!"

"How so?" she entertained the notion.

"Sleep driving? Give me a break! That's not even a real thing!"

"It absolutely is. It's not common, but it happens. There was a man in the late 80's who drove to his in-laws in his sleep. He killed his mother-in-law and nearly killed his father-in-law," she stared at me with conviction and I stared back in disbelief. "Look it up!" she added.

I continued to stare at her as the story grew in familiarity. I remembered reading something about that a long time ago, but I had completely forgot about it until she refreshed my memory.

"Anyway, thanks to me, and your sleep driving skills, you made it home safely before you had a chance to go back down the path both you and I know you don't want to go down again."

I was floored. I didn't know what to say. What could I say? All of these new emotions and questions swept over me; confusion, fear, anger, uncertainty. Was what she was saying true? Did she really guide me home safely in my dreams? Was she my guardian angel? My gaze stayed both focused and lost on nothing in front of me, my eyes wide in a tranced gaze. I stood there, frozen, for what seemed like an eternity. I didn't know what was next. What do I do? What do I say? Was I going crazy?

"You're not going crazy," she assured me.

My head didn't move, but my eyes fixed to hers. "Then how the fuck did you just do that?"

"You had other questions?" Sea asked, still smiling.

She was right. Her demeanor pulled the reigns on the conversation and almost forced me to obey. Without waiting for an answer to that question, I asked another against my own will. "How did my wife know I was at the bar?"

"I guess you could call it 'a wife's intuition.'" Her smile seemed mocking now.

I threw daggers at her from my eyes which seemed to do her no harm, but she got the hint that I didn't like that answer.

"Let's just say a little birdie told her you were there that night."

"No, let's not 'just say.' I want to know how she knew I was at the bar. And I want to know how you knew that she knew I was at the bar." It was all getting very confusing. I wasn't even sure I was wording my questions right anymore. "How do you know all of this?" She still never told me WHAT she was.

"I'll tell you WHAT I am some day; when the time is right."

"The time is right; right now. Tell me," I demanded.

"No. Wouldn't you rather know why I don't blame your wife for cheating on you?"

I had no idea where that came from; more importantly, I had no idea she felt that way. But that was quite the redirection because the burning desire I had to learn of her origins quickly extinguished as a new fire began to burn inside me. What the hell did she mean by that?

"What?"

"I don't really blame your wife for what she did."

"Oh," I belittled as I crossed my arms, "This should be good."

"The sun never touches the rainbows it creates."

I curled my fingers like I was holding a ball in each hand and pointed them upwards in a sign of frustration. "Why are you always so cryptic when you talk? Can you elaborate please?"

"You and your wife created the love you share, right?"

"I guess."

"So, that love can't be possessed, by either one of you; it can only be appreciated."

She still wasn't making sense, but I thought maybe she was onto something. "Go on," I allowed.

"So you, the sun, can't physically touch or 'possess' the love, the rainbow, that you two share. However, in the case of someone who has anxiety and insecurity issues," she presented me with her hands, "that person may feel inadequate or incomplete without being able to touch it. So, in turn, that person becomes physically possessive of the other; treating that person almost like a piece of property, as a substitute for the inability to touch the rainbow you've created. Does that make sense?"

"I think so," I said sheepishly. "So, let me get this straight: You're saying I'm supposed to appreciate my wife and the relationship I have with her, but because of my own issues and an unconscious need to actually physically touch and hold the love we have, I instead become possessive of her?"

"Precisely," she said with her smile.

I thought about it and nodded slowly. "Possibly, but explain why she brought up the fact that I'm always in my own head at my last counseling session with her? That has nothing to do with possession. I'm just so mentally distant from her, she claims that's what drove us apart."

"You're being possessive of yourself to spite her. You're taking control of all aspects of the marriage so she has none. But she doesn't want control; she just wants to lay with you and enjoy the rainbow again. You're letting your insecurities get the best of you instead of sharing the rainbow with her. So, in light of that, no, I don't think she was to blame for cheating on you. You gave her no other choice."

"What about divorce?" I suggested.

"And let the sun set to diminish that rainbow forever? She doesn't want that. She's holding onto the hope that one day you'll see the rainbow for what it's worth again. In the meantime, she's her own person, free to do whatever she pleases. She's not your possession; you're not in charge of what she does. Even through marriage; that wasn't a purchase, that was a celebration to solidify the rainbow you two created 'until death do you part.' It's her choice whether or not she decides to sleep with someone else. And if you can start yourself over and begin to appreciate the rainbow again, the 'choice' is no longer an option to her."

"So, I should just let her go around and fuck whoever she wants?" I offered childishly.

"Essentially, yes." She considered what she was saying. "Well, yes and no. You should leave her to make her own choices; she IS her own person after all. If you give yourself up to her, just a little, the rewards will be great. If you forfeit control and stop letting your insecurities consume you, she won't have any need or desire to seek either physical or emotional connections with anyone else."

I heard what she was saying; it was beginning to make sense, but her deep philosophical knowledge was overwhelmingly sexy and I found myself getting lost in my attraction to her. Her implications and intentions were having the exact opposite effect on me. There was something drawing me to her inexplicably and before I could even realize what it was, I found my lips locked onto hers, drawing out a long and passionate kiss.

There was nothing but magic in that moment; I let my tongue into her mouth, but only briefly before retracting it. She did the same as we slowly swiveled our heads back and forth, gently locking our hands; mine on her neck and hers in my hair. The waves stopped crashing and everything stood still, even my heartbeat. My hands slowly made their way down the outline of her body until they rested on her hips and I pulled my lips off hers.

I rested my forehead on hers and stared into her eyes, enjoying the rush that was still coursing through me while trying to figure out the familiarity that was that kiss. Her lips, her tongue, her taste, the way she moved throughout it; I had kissed her before, but where?

"What was that?" I asked.

"A kiss," she said with that smile; that beautiful smile.

"Obviously," I chuckled. "Why did it taste so familiar? When have I kissed you before?"

"Oh, the things you wish you knew. Why don't we just enjoy it for what it was? A kiss."

"Because…" I couldn't believe what I was about to say, "the feeling I had while we were kissing was the same feeling…" I couldn't even finish my sentence.

"I know," she said.

"No, you don't know. That's the exact same feeling I had when I first met my wife. Such an incredible feeling. In fact, I think it felt even better this time. I can't believe I'm saying this because I still have no idea if you're even real, but I think I'm falling..." I laughed. "That's so stupid; I don't even know anything about you! But it just feels so right, you know? It's like I've known you forever! It's like you're everything I've ever wanted in a partner and then some! It's so hard to explain that feeling, you know?"

"I know," she repeated.

"I know, it sounds stupid," I said.

"No. If you had any idea, you'd understand."

"What do you mean?" I asked.

"Don't worry about it. Just do me a favor?" she requested.

"Yeah, of course! Anything!" My will was at her command now.

"Just promise me you won't bring me up in conversation to anyone; not your therapist, not your wife, especially not your wife. Nobody!"

"I promise," I offered with a playful grin.

"I mean it!" she demanded.

"I won't tell anyone," I reassured her. And then, just like that, I woke up.

15

Let me paint you another picture: There's a constant metronome of beeping at precisely seventy-four beats per minute. All of the walls are a nauseating white. There's a window along the far wall that lets in a considerable amount of sunlight, giving the impression that all is so well with the world when indeed it is not. There's a small bedside table that they stuff all of your belongings into. There's a tray on wheels that's holding what's left of today's dinner special of slop and jello. An IV pole is staged to one side of the bed and displays a drip bag for hydration. An array of various tubes, hoses, wires, and medical contraptions decorate the room throughout and set a very clinical ambience on the medical prison cell. At the center of the room, there's a hospital bed, and there I lay.

The IV is plugged into my arm, the pads and wires for the heart tests they've performed are stuck to my chest, and the reality of the trauma I just went through is finally setting in. I had the back of my hand resting on my forehead and my eyes closed, trying to rest, when I heard commotion coming from the door. I opened my eyes just enough to make out what was going on and turned my head steadily towards the door.

A middle-aged man with salt-and-peppered hair and a long white coat entered and made his way to my bed. He had reading glasses down to the tip of his nose that he was looking through to examine the clipboard and medical file he was holding. After making peace with what he was studying, he looked up at me over his glasses and said, "It's time for your CT scan. Let's see if we can figure out what's going on."

I closed my eyes and nodded gingerly. My thought process wasn't operating the way it usually was; everything was cloudy. No obsessing, no anxiety, no Sea, no thoughts really; I was dead in my own mind. If I were trapped on that island again, I'd be lost and running in circles in a thick cloud of fog. What a scary feeling it is to be unaware.

The doctor and a couple of nurses carted me down in my hospital bed to a room on the opposite end of the hospital. I entered the room and picked my head up briefly to see what was going on. There, in the center of the room, was a large machine that looked like a giant donut with a long table protruding from the middle. Everything else about the room was mundane. Nothing else existed and the walls were painted white; clinical paradise.

My bed was wheeled over and lined up next to the bed attached to the scanner. The workers gave a three count and heave-ho'd me onto the scanner bed with ease.

"How are you feeling?" the doctor asked.

I closed my eyes and nodded slowly again.

"There's a room attached to this one that I'll be in," he explained. "I'll be working on a computer that collects all of the data from this scanner. I can hear everything that goes on in here. If you need anything, just let me know; I can communicate with you through an intercom. Do you have any questions?"

I forgot my commands for a moment and nodded briefly. Once I realized that was the wrong response, I furled my eyebrows and slowly rotated my head from side to side. On that note, my doctor left me in silence with the scanner.

After deliberate and prolonged tinkering on the computer, the scanner began to make a faint whirring sound. Through the intercom, my doctor continued his lecture. "Can you hear me?" he asked. I responded with another steady head nod.

"Great. The platform you're on is going to start heading for the donut shortly. It can be a somewhat uncomfortable experience, but it's not like an MRI where you're completely enclosed. On my command, at certain points throughout the procedure, I'll need you to hold your breath for me until I say it's ok to breathe. Just relax and try to keep your mind off of the scanner and you should be ok. Do you have any questions or concerns?"

I, again, shook my head to confirm.

"Are you ready to begin?"

I nodded. I heard the motor for the table kick into gear and felt myself start to move towards the donut. My anxiety started up a little bit, so I took my doctor's advice. My mind began to drift and I reflected on the events that led to my being in a hospital in the first place.

When I woke up from my kiss with Sea, my mind was in paradise. Thoughts of my cheating wife weren't even a particle in the wondrous visions that danced in my head. My new obsession was just how incredible Sea was. Everything about this woman was amazing; it was no issue that I could only be with her in my dreams; I would figure something out. The outside air was painted with beautiful blues and greens as I pranced to my car to make way to my next counseling session.

"Sing my song, Daddy." I looked in the rearview mirror and met eyes with my little JellyBean, smiling and beaming like usual. I smiled back and nodded. You know the song, but I know you loved it so much, I'll put the words here for you to always remember:

I'll love you in the morning

I'll love you in the evening
I'll love you when the sun is bright

I'll love you in the afternoon
And in the beautiful display
Of all the stars at night

I'll love you at breakfast
I'll love you at lunch
I'll even love you at dinnertime

I'll love you with all my love
My love is yours
I know your love is mine

That was about as far as I got before my wife got into the car. "Do you remember where it's at?" she asked.

"The people we've both known pretty much our whole lives? Yes, I think I'm familiar." Our babysitters during our session today were our lifelong friends who had twins of their own. The fact that my wife was questioning my knowledge of where they lived blew my mind.

We made it to our friends place and then over to the therapist's office with time to spare. He greeted us in the waiting room and we followed him into his office, sat down, and attempted to make more headway into the relationship.

I was in such a great place mentally during this session. My compliance throughout surprised my wife and my therapist and to be honest, I kind of surprised myself, too.

"You seem to be in a really good mood today," my therapist pointed out.

"Yeah, I guess I am," I admitted.

"Do you care to discuss it?" he asked.

"Discuss what?"

"Why you're so happy today?"

"Is that a crime? That I be happy?"

"Well, no, but you've been so graveled and distant since the day you started coming in. It's a nice change of pace."

"I guess sometimes it takes an outside influence to realize how great life is." Whoops. I realized what I was implying, but I hoped they didn't catch on to my subtle cues.

"What do you mean?" my wife asked.

"What do you mean?" I asked, but realized I was just repeating.

"What outside influence are you talking about?" she interrogated.

I didn't know what to say. I know Sea told me to keep her existence a secret, so I couldn't divulge any information about her. I had to think fast. I hesitated at first, but I saved myself rather smoothly.

"I sang my song to JellyBean today. I hadn't done that in awhile. It's such a positive song; sends such a positive message. It's just so positive. It's a positive song. Positive." My argument was shallow, and I didn't think it was going to hold up considering their faces.

"It really is a good song," my wife shot the counselor a smile.

"What is it?" he inquired.

"It's just this song he randomly sang for our JellyBean when she was born. He just kind of pulled it out of thin air, but it's so beautiful, and he sings it to her all the time."

"Mind if I hear it?"

I shot my wife a look, but realized this was all my fault for opening my big mouth. "I suppose," I surrendered. I cleared my throat and gave him my best rendition of the song.

He had nothing but good things to say about the contents of the song and we discussed, at length, its origins and its implications on my relationship with my daughter and my family. He tried tying the song into the fabric of what my family represents and while it made sense, I still had Sea on the brain and I couldn't help but keep coming back to my strong feelings towards her and my lack of intimacy and interest to my wife.

After thoughtful deliberation with myself, I realized I had to disregard the pact I made with Sea. I had to tell my wife what was going on. I didn't know how I was going to do it, but I needed to at least put my new found feelings out there on the table so they could be discussed.

"I can't do this," I finally admitted. The room fell silent. The happy expressions painted on both the counselor's and my wife's faces fell off. They knew something else was going on.

"What do you mean?" my wife asked.

"Yeah, what's going on? Please," my therapist insisted.

There was a long silence as I tried to gather the words to express what I was feeling and who I was feeling it for. Once I chose my words carefully, I began my monologue.

"There's someone else," I started. My wife took a breath in and opened her mouth to talk, but I threw up a hand to stop her before she started.

"I don't know where to start," I continued. "I'm still making sense of it all myself. What started out as an innocent interaction has turned into something more."

"Who is she?" my wife interrupted.

"You don't know her," I admitted.

"Someone from your office," she declared. "I knew it."

"No, it's not someone from the office," I reassured her. "I WISH it was someone from the office."

"What's THAT supposed to mean?" she demanded.

"It's so much more complicated than that." Beyond those words, we started to talk at the same time and battled to talk over one another until the therapist got in the middle and brought the room to silence. After a pause, I let off the dynamite.

"She's in my dreams."

My wife looked at me with both disgust and confusion. "What?" she whispered.

"The woman I've been talking to: she's in my dreams. Her name's Sea and I…"

My wife enunciated her next sentence. "What. The fuck. Are you talking about?"

I felt deflated. I completely came undone. What WAS I talking about? None of this made sense, but at the same time it felt so right. I met a woman in my dreams. This woman had been giving me life advice and coaching me to help me get passed my wife's recent affair. In the meantime, I developed feelings for this imaginary woman, or whatever the fuck she was. And amidst all of the craziness and nonsensical scenarios I had been confronted with, both in my life and in my dreams, I felt fine in the comfort that existed in talking with Sea when I did. It made no sense, none whatsoever, but I finally admitted it to myself. I loved her.

"I love her," I said to myself. Tears started to escape from the corners of my wife's eyes.

"Who?" she demanded, completely disregarding the fact that she was to blame for all of this. She was the one who cheated on me in the first place! She was the one who unravelled my entire being and made me question who I am. She, in turn, made Sea, whoever she was, come into my dreams and help me through what my wife had done to me. Everything that had transpired up to this point was all due to my wife's actions. I can't help it if Sea was everything I wanted in a partner! She was perfect! I was done dwelling on what to say, so I just said it.

"Sea."

"What?" my wife had a disgusted look on her face. "See? See what?"

"Her name's Sea," I cut her off.

"Who the fuck is Sea?" she sounded distressed, but I didn't care anymore. She had a question, so I made my best attempt to answer. In my efforts, however, my words began to jumble together. I tried to speak in sentences, but everything sounded like I was talking passed a mouthful of marbles. My wife's disgusted expression quickly turned to concern as she ran towards me and threw my arm around her head to keep me from falling over. My face felt numb, but I had no way of communicating this, since my speech was shot.

She scooped me up by the arm and attempted to keep me on my feet. I couldn't hear her, but I saw my wife look over at the therapist in a panic and her mouth form the words, "He's having a stroke!"

I was so scared by what was going on; it was such a rush and I didn't know how to process all of it. There's not much I remember from that point. I kept trying to talk to my wife, but I couldn't form any words to save my life. My vision went blurry and shortly after I faded to black.

16

I was still in a haze when the results of my scan came back. I could almost feel a new barrage of questions trying to infiltrate my brain, but there was nothing more than a pile of mush in its place; nowhere the questions could possibly go.

"This has never happened before," the doctor started. "Are you sure you're recounting what happened to the best of your abilities?" The question was directed toward my wife.

"Yes, absolutely," my wife insisted. "He had a stroke."

"He didn't have a stroke," the doctor corrected her. This piqued my interest, so I peeled my eyes open slowly and shifted my head toward the doctor.

What was supposed to come out as,"What?" simply expressed itself as "Whhaaaaa…" It didn't have a chance to completely roll off my tongue before my doctor cut me off.

"You didn't have a stroke. You're a medical anomaly. We have no idea what happened to you. You've passed every test we've administered with flying colors. You're as healthy as a horse. Everything you experienced at your therapist was a clear cut indication that you had a stroke, but…"

"But what?" my wife cut him off.

Doc opened his mouth, but no words came out, so he closed it and shook his head.

"We'd like to keep you for another day or two to try and pinpoint exactly what's going on," he explained.

"If he's healthy as a horse, what could possibly be going on?" my wife demanded.

"That's what we'd like to pinpoint." My wife wanted to continue arguing, but realized she had no ammo. She looked at him with her mouth open trying to find the right combination of words to say for a few seconds, then dropped her head in defeat.

I, again, tried forming some vocabulary from behind a garbled mouth, but had no luck. Doc looked at me with sympathy and patience until he accepted that I wouldn't be saying anything that made sense. His sympathetic look shifted to my wife as he said, "I'm sorry," and he walked out of the room.

"Oh, babe," my wife said.

Of course I had no words to deliver, but if I could, it would have been a simple, "Save it." So, instead, I closed my eyes and turned my head away. I was so far beyond even speaking to my wife, I almost felt a sense of unnecessary physical pain from the thought.

I could feel her staring at me, probably trying to find some more, relevant, words to say.

"Here," she finally said, placing something on the table beside me that made a rattle. I looked over and saw a pill bottle; some kind of pill bottle.

"Sleeping pills," she informed me. "I figured you wouldn't be able to sleep and they wouldn't give you anything for it, so…"

I closed my eyes again and nodded slowly.

"I still want to know who…" my hand went up in her direction and interrupted her. I didn't want to hear it. I just had a stroke, regardless of what the doctor said, and I wasn't in the mood to argue with her about irrelevant bullshit.

I glanced at her and she had her lips pursed. I stared at her while I pointed to the door. She stared back as tears began to collect in her eyes. When she realized it was useless to say anything else, she stormed out.

I laid in my bed and tried to collect any thoughts I could fabricate. I mulled over the doctor's diagnosis of what had happened to me. "...wasn't a stroke..." What was it, then? I'd never had a stroke and I, of course, was no doctor, but all signs pointed to one. I may have been safe from the perils of a stroke, but the suspense was killing me.

My mind shifted focus to my wife. What was I going to do about my wife? Everything we had done together, everything we've been through, and it all came down to this. I drilled my brain for far too long about the whole relationship and what it recently became: nothing more than a tree whittled into a toothpick. There was nothing left to fight for. I had given up and lost all hope. I thought that would be hard to swallow, but I found solace in the mere thought of Sea.

What was I going to do about Sea? I wanted to be with her, but she only existed in my dreams. How was I going to make that work? Should I just take a bunch of sleeping pills and trap myself in a slumber forever? That would work; and it would allow me to be with Sea.

I laughed to myself and quickly pushed the thought from my mind. My wife left me with a bottle of pills. I turned my head and looked at the bottle. She left those here for me. Maybe somewhere, deep down, she wanted this for me. She heard me say Sea was in my dreams after all. Maybe, subconsciously, she really wants me to be happy and left these in hopes that I would take enough to be with Sea and be truly happy.

I continued to stare at the bottle while these thoughts processed. I'm not sure if those were my wife's intentions, but the more I toyed with the notion, the more is sounded like a spectacular plan. My heart started to race as I kept pushing myself and convincing myself to just do it. Finally, I crept over and reached for the bottle, a sweet release to this life finally in my grasp. I eased back onto the bed and turned the bottle in my hand so I could read the label.

I looked back at the counter where they were, confused about just what was going on. Was I overreacting? Whatever happened to me at the therapist's office, was it beginning to just manifest itself as some manic episode?

I turned to put the bottle back where it went, shook my head, and retracted my body back to my bed. I needed to do this; it was the only way. I was being manic, I wasn't being fucking dramatic; this was the only thing I could do to make me feel better. For closure, peace of mind, and for eternal happiness.

I slowly twisted the cap and turned the bottle over into my palm. I rattled the bottle as seven, eight, nine, ten pills fell out. Without replacing the lid, I tossed the bottle over the side of my bed as I heard the bottle crash and the remaining pills scatter across the floor. I stared at my palm as I picked up the glass of water from my bed tray.

I started to well up as I considered everything I was leaving behind to be happy. My job, my wife, you. Oh God; that thought alone sent me over the edge. I threw my hand over my mouth before I had any more time to think and back down from what was surely the only solution to my happiness. Tears flooded my cheeks as I took gulp after gulp, counting every pill as it made its way to my stomach.

I swallowed the last pill and took a few more drinks before I set the glass down. I collapsed my head onto my pillow and stared at the ceiling, gently sobbing as I reflected on what I had just done. I forced myself to remember why I was doing it: I want to be with Sea. My wife ruined my life, and I want to be with Sea. My wife ruined my life, and I want to be with Sea. My wife ruined my life, and I...

Before I had a chance to repeat it again, I was knocked off my bed and began falling.

17

Something was off about the island this time; something just didn't feel right. There was almost a static in the air; an audible static. It was still grayscale, but everything was hazy, almost like… static. It all looked distorted; now that I think about it, it looked like a TV station with a poor signal. That's exactly what it looked like. The island was disconnecting from my psyche.

Horizontal lines cast from one side of my vision to the other pulled the scenery into opposite directions. I began to run towards the shoreline, but it never seemed to get closer. When I looked down at my feet, I noticed I was running in place. I dropped to the ground and crumbled myself into a little ball. The anger and terror that started in my brain started to fill my whole body and take over.

This wasn't how things were supposed to go; the island wasn't supposed to be like this. I was supposed to stay on this island forever without a worry and enjoy my time with…

"Sea!" I looked up from my crouched position and shouted for her. I looked to my left and to my right, but no sign of her. I turned and dropped my hip to the sand to look off into what was behind me, which was now to my left.

"Sea!" I shouted again. I kept scanning all around me, but it was hard to look at the island in the condition it was in. I turned my body back around so I was on my knees, dropped my forearms onto the sand, and drove my head into my hands.

"Noooooo!" I cried out. This was all too overwhelming. I didn't know what to do. Was I trapped?

"No," a voice called out from right in front of me. I looked up to see it was finally Sea.

"'No' what?" I asked cynically.

"Why… do…" she stuttered. Her voice was breaking up badly, just like a… yeah, like a TV station with a poor signal.

"What?" My cynicism was wiped away by concern as I came to my feet.

"Where… I… even…"

I shook my head. "I can't understand you!"

"Sleeping… darkness…"

I didn't know what to do at this point. I was so confused by what was going on and a fog started to set in on the island.

"I love…" I tried to finish my thought as I went in to hug Sea, but instead of hugging her, I ended up hugging myself. I passed right through her. She, or the image of what I thought was her, became distorted upon my contact. She was just a mirage. Was she just a mirage this whole time? She was just a fabrication of my fucked up mind, and in that moment I was content with myself for taking those sleeping pills and accepted my fate on this island, or whatever was to become of me.

"Goodbye," I whispered to her, and I turned around and sprinted to the water. I really didn't know what I was doing, it just felt right. Water sloshed at my feet as I crashed into the shoreline. The sudden resistance from the waves brought me to my knees. I scurried back to my feet and lightning flashed across the sky, followed by a thunderous boom that reverberated throughout my entire being.

A downpour fell from the sky and I tipped my head back and closed my eyes to feel the cold pellets ricochet off my face. It was such a… clean feeling. Is this what death feels like? Every emotion came rushing to the front of my consciousness and I peeled my now-soaked shirt off of my body. I arched my back and looked up to the sky, letting the rain shower over my face and my chest as I let out a scream.

"Aaahhhhhhhhh!" It was so liberating; such a good feeling of just letting go. I did it again.

"Aaaaahhhhhhhhhhhhh!" Light began to scatter and I fell to my knees, the water reaching just above my belly button. I sank my chin to my chest and sat there, unmoving. I thought of everything my life had become; this mistake I let go on for too long. I thought of my wife and everything we had been through. I thought of how I let it all slip away. I thought of Sea and how I died for her; how I died for someone that doesn't exist. But mostly, I thought of you: I thought of how I let you down. I thought of everything I'd miss seeing because I messed everything up. I thought of what I'd do if I could go back and change things. I thought of what I would do if I had just one more chance with my wife. I'd tell her I love her and that I was a changed man. I'd tell her I'd never let her go, but it was all too late now; too late for all of that. My time had come and gone; this was my happy ending.

The rain continued to fall, but it's sound slowly turned into a faint heartbeat. I looked up to see the light scattering some more. I got back on my feet and slowly started back toward the horizon. It was hard to stand anymore; not enough energy to go on. I stopped and stared straight ahead. It was hard to tell whether the water on my face was rain or tears. It didn't matter anymore; I just decided it was time to watch everything end. The horizon was beginning to fade and the heart beat slower and slower. Everything turned to black as the heartbeat simultaneously ended. All was darkness; nothingness. I lifted my hands to look at my palms but saw nothing. Everything was… nothing.

18

"He's stable now."

I was awoken by the commotion of people talking around me. I opened my eyes, but couldn't see anything.

"What?" I asked.

"But he's going to be OK?" I heard a woman's voice ask.

"What's going on? Where am I?" I demanded.

"He's going to be fine," I heard another voice say; a man's voice this time.

"Someone fucking talk to me!" I screamed. The woman began sobbing.

"Why can't I see anything?!" My impatience was growing; coupled with my anxiety.

"All we can do now is wait," the man's voice said.

"Wait for what? What's going on?" I couldn't figure out why nobody was responding to me or if they could even hear me, so I sat in silence.

"Wait for what? How many sleeping pills did he swallow? And we just wait for that to course through his system?" the woman's voice said.

"Yes and no," started the man. "His body digested most of the pills he swallowed. We were able to go in and pump out what was still undigested. His body is under a lot of stress as a result of trying to metabolize that much at one time. The sleeping pills are doing their job of exciting thr GABA receptors to promote sleep. So now, we wait..." The woman must've shown a face of confusion; there was a moment of silence that the man broke with, "for his body to digest the pills and get through his sleep cycle."

It was ironic that he was discussing this; his voice started to fade away and I was beginning to hear the sweet lull of waves crashing onto a gray shoreline.

I was waiting for a rush of feelings to come over me, but my body was so out of tune; nothing came about. I opened my eyes and turned my head to confirm that I was, in fact, back on the island. The gray oasis presented itself to me, so I looked back up to the sky and closed my eyes, accepting that numb would be the only feeling I'd be experiencing from here on out.

I even tried to process thoughts; no luck there either. I just laid there and let the sounds of the island encapsulate my eardrums.

I noticed there was no static this time around; I tried to wonder what that was about. A lack of thoughts brought me back to square one.

"Why did you do that?" a voice said behind me. I knew who it was, so I didn't bother opening my eyes. I just laid still like I was working on a tan, which was comical considering the infinite cloud cover.

There was a long pause before I answered with, "Do what?"

"Why did you take those pills?" This was a different Sea this time. Both anger and concern joined her words.

Another long pause was broken with a very chopped and almost incomprehensible, "I don't know."

"What do you mean?" she asked.

A smile broke on my face; her Mona Lisa smile.

"The tables have turned," I sneered.

"This isn't a fucking joke." Her cursing instantly wiped my face clean of condescendence. This was huge; in all of the time I've known Sea, however short, she's NEVER cursed at me or to me. It reminded me of my wife. This must've been a serious offense in her eyes. I started to come to life a little bit as I came up onto my elbows.

"What?" I didn't know what else to say. What was there to say? I took those sleeping pills to be with Sea. There was no other viable solution at that point. My plan was to take the pills, put myself into a coma or worse (better), the sweet release, and be with Sea forever.

"It doesn't work that way," replied Sea to my thoughts.

"How do you do that?!" I argued. I needed answers!

"You can't just take sleeping pills and expect to be with me. It doesn't work like that!"

"I... what?" The conversation shifted to her advantage again.

"When you take sleeping pills, there's nothingness in your subconscious. You don't experience REM sleep; you don't experience anything! That's why the island was crumbling the way it was. As the pills were being metabolized and started coursing through your veins, this island, your subconscious, began to break down and fall apart. If you want to be with me, taking sleeping pills is not the answer."

"But I took sleeping pills before; the first night I actually saw you. Explain that!"

"You took vitamins," she said.

I just stared at her. "What?" I said finally. "Noooo, I took sleeping pills, I remember I..."

"Those were vitamins," she cut me off. "Next time you're awake, check your medicine cabinet. Your wife puts multivitamins next to the sleeping pills. You were so tired that night, you weren't paying attention to the bottle you grabbed, but you picked up the bottle of multivitamins and took a handful of those."

"Then why did I fall asleep so quickly?" I quizzed her.

"Placebo effect," she said matter-of-factly.

My God, she was good. I was falling for her harder every minute.

"So, what, then?" I finally asked.

"What 'what'?" she rebuttaled.

"If I can't take sleeping pills to be with you? What, then? What do I need to do to be with you?"

She mulled the suggestion over for a minute.

"If you want to be with me…" she paused and began pacing. I, naturally, followed her lead, and we found ourselves pacing the shoreline. I was surprisingly silent while I waited patiently for her to give me something to work with. We walked about a quarter mile before she spoke up again.

"Take her out on a date."

"Who?" It was more of a rhetorical question. Something to say to fill the silence. I knew who she was talking about; And that wasn't an option.

"Your wife."

"Absolutely not."

"Why not?"

"I don't want to be with her. I don't love her anymore. There's no point in even associating myself with her anymore."

"Then what's the harm in taking her to dinner?"

She had a point. I considered the notion in my head for a moment.

"Ok. I'll take my wife out to dinner. I'll treat her to say goodbye. And then what?"

"You'll see."

"I'll see what?"

"You both have to get dressed up," she ignored my question again.

I scoffed in my head. "I can do that."

"You have to treat her like you still love her."

"But how can I…"

"You still love her," she repeated, stopping me mid-sentence.

"No I don't, I…"

"And you'll kiss her at the end of the date," her impatience with me was starting to wear through her Mona Lisa smile.

"I'm not kissing her!" I exclaimed.

"You'll kiss her at the end of the date," she repeated. "And not just a peck on the cheek. You need to kiss her with passion; like the way you kissed me that night."

I had forgot about that night in the midst of our negotiations. The thought put a smile on my face; it went as quickly as it came.

"You have my word," I surrendered. "And then I can be with you?"

"You'll see," she repeated.

"See what?" I demanded. She said nothing else. Her smile was the last thing I saw before I was awoken by the electric equivalent of my heartbeat.

19

"Why are you smiling?" A voice in my room shook me out of my tranquil state. I shot an accidental glare at my wife to figure where the voice was coming from. When I made sense of my world again, I rested my head back on my pillow and closed my eyes.

"Nothing," I said finally.

"It's nice seeing you smile," she admitted.

"Yeah, well…" I had nothing else to say.

"How are you feeling?" she asked. I just nodded slowly. There was a silence, so I turned to look at my wife again. Her eyes were beginning to well up as she tried to find the right combination of words to say.

"Why did you… the pills… why… what did I…" Nothing seemed to fit together properly. I didn't have the heart to tell her why I did it, so, in proper Sea fashion, I ignored her need to know; I should utilize the same practice on myself.

"I want to take you out to dinner."

"What?" I knew she asked because I threw her off-guard with the question, but I took it as an expression of her disapproval of the way I asked. Where are my manners?

"I'm sorry," I corrected myself. "May I take you out to dinner?"

The smile that came across her face could've lit the darkest cave.

"I..." she looked down at the floor. I don't know what she was thinking about, but before I had time to consider it, she looked back up at me with an answer. "Yes!"

I smiled back at her with the most energy I could find at the time.

"Let's get me out of here, first. I'm ready to go home."

"You still need to rest, but I'll be here in the meantime." She sat down in the chair beside me, her eyes fixed on me, and held my hand as we waited for any other news the doctors would bring us. I'm still not sure what happened to me, but my main focus was to get this dinner over with and get on with my life.

It had been a week since I was out of the hospital, and enough time had passed that I was feeling particularly stellar. I straightened myself up in the mirror; I regularly wore a suit for work, but it had been awhile since I "dressed to the nines" and I was feeling exceptionally special tonight.

I grappled the knot on my tie one more time before I popped my arms in front of me to straighten my sleeves and nodded to myself in the mirror. A smirk shone across my face and I walked towards the door.

Before I had a chance to walk through, I was stopped in my tracks by an angel. My wife looked more stunning than she had in... in a long time.

I'm not up to snuff on lady fashion, so I'll explain what she was wearing to the best of my abilities: it was a red dress... I don't know what else to say. It had those spaghetti straps on her shoulders and it came down to her knees. It was a low cut v-shape on the top and she didn't fit into it; it fit onto her. She was the definition of cutting edge perfection.

"Wow." It was the only thing I could think to say; I was speechless.

Apparently she was, too, as her response was nothing more than a bashful smile as she pulled a tuft of hair behind her ear and looked down at her shoes. Oh, she was wearing heels, too. I hadn't noticed them at first; I was too drawn in by everything else. I was ravished.

I motioned towards the door. "Shall we?"

She nodded vigorously in approval. We walked out the door, got into my car, and I whisked us away to the restaurant.

The ride there was silent; not awkward silent, but more like first date silent. What was there to talk about? I was torn: on the one hand, my wife looked incredible. On the other, I was just doing all of this so I could be with Sea. The butterflies in my stomach were doing cartwheels.

I took my eyes off the road for a moment to admire her. She really was beautiful; made me forget everything we had recently been through. But I needed to keep my mind on the task at hand! I shot my glance back on the drive. Out of the corner of my eye, I saw her look over, smile, and look back down at her hands in her lap. This was starting to fuck with me.

We made it to the restaurant and one valet driver took my place behind the wheel as the other opened the door for my wife. I met her on her side of the car, presented my arm to her, she hooked hers onto mine, and we walked inside with a warm embrace. What was happening?

"Good evening!" greeted the host. "Welcome to pinacle de l'âme! How many will we be seating tonight?"

"Uh," I briefly forgot how to speak. "Just two."

The host nodded politely. "Right this way!"

I allowed my wife to walk in front of me. She held my hand behind her the whole way. I was so stunned by her, I forgot we were walking, where we were walking to, where we were at, everything. All that existed was her. My feelings for my wife began rushing back, but I knew what I needed to do, so instead of acting on them, I swallowed them.

We got to our table and the host pulled the seat out for my wife.

"Oh," she said in surprise. She straightened the backside of her dress and helped the host scoot her in. "Thank you," she said.

I sat myself and the host presented our menus to us. "Your server will be right with you."

I really wish I could tell you what the restaurant looked like, but I couldn't remember for two reasons: I hadn't eaten all day, and my wife's beauty continued to take my breathe away. So, my mind kept shifting back and forth between food and my wife. All the way to our table, my mind was on my wife. As soon as we were handed our menus, my mind was on food. What I can tell you about the restaurant is that the table was just big enough for two, and there was a candle lit in the center, which seemed to be the only light emanating from the restaurant in general.

"Good evening," said our server. "My name is such & such," can't remember his name, on account of being lost in my wife, "I'll be your server for the evening. Can I get you started with something to drink?"

"I'll have a Cabernet Sauv…" she trailed her words and looked at me, disappointment in herself shone on her face. I shook my head with permission; a kind of, "no, don't be disappointed." She looked back up and said, "Just a house Cabernet will be fine."

"And for you, sir?"

"Just a water will be fine," I said with a smile.

"Very well, I'll be right back." He bowed slightly and excused himself.

I went back to the menu, trying to decide what sounded good; it all sounded good. Do I want pasta or some type of meat and side? Do I want chicken or beef? Or do I want land or sea? Sea. The name clouded my mind with her presence. Her request began to repeat in my head. "You'll kiss her at the end of the date, and not just a peck on the cheek. You need to kiss her with passion; like the way you kissed me that night."

I continued to browse the menu, not really looking at anything, just thinking about what Sea said. I looked over the menu to my wife. She was browsing her own menu; I wondered if she had something else on her mind as well. She must've felt me staring, as she looked up from her menu and we locked eyes. In unison, we folded our menu's and placed them on the table, our stare unbroken. The server returned rather quickly with the Cab and the water.

"For tonight's specials," he started as he placed our drinks in front of us. "We have…"

I threw up my hand to interrupt him, still not breaking my gaze on my wife. He stared at me for a moment, glanced over to my wife, and then back at me.

"Sir?" he wondered.

"Can you just… give us a moment?" I requested. I fell back in my back, my gaze not dying.

"Very well. I'll give you some time." Again, he bowed and excused himself.

We continued to stare at each other. And she stared at me. And I stared at her. And finally she asked, "What?"

I didn't say anything, but I started to well up.

"What?" she demanded with a little more conviction this time.

And that was when I realized it. I couldn't go through with this. I couldn't sit here through this whole date, reconnecting with my wife, reminiscing the past, catching up with her, and not fall in love with her all over again. I couldn't do it. I wanted to be with Sea and that was my final decision. I needed to do what I had to do to fulfill Sea's requests so I could be with her. I couldn't wait until the end of the date; I needed to kiss her now.

I pushed my chair back and stood up, finally breaking the lock from my wife.

"Stand up," I said.

"What?"

"I said stand up." Tears began streaming down my face.

"Babe, you're scaring me."

"Just do it," I sobbed. She swallowed hard and cautiously pushed her chair back. She stood up slowly and we met halfway. I grabbed her by her shoulders, gently, and stared at her again. I started to softly weep, as the reality of everything finally hit me. I could say it a thousand times; she was so beautiful and I was starting to see the woman I had fallen in love with all of those years ago. This would be the single most hardest thing I'd ever have to do. But it was now or never. If I didn't do this, I knew I'd be miserable the rest of my life. I closed my eyes and leaned forward to kiss her.

I let my tongue into her mouth, but only briefly before retracting it. She did the same as we slowly swiveled our heads back and forth; my hands slowly shifted from her shoulders and locked onto her neck and she locked hers in my hair. Nothing else existed in the moment, except her, myself, and my heartbeat. My hands slowly made their way down the outline of her body until they rested on her hips and I pulled my lips off hers.

I rested my forehead on hers and stared into her eyes, enjoying the rush that was still coursing through me as I finally realized the familiarity of the kiss I had with Sea. It was my wife's kisses; all this time. It had been so long since we had a kiss like that that I had forgotten what it felt like. So long that when Sea and I kissed, I couldn't even pinpoint where I had tasted it before.

I wrapped my arms around my wife, I held her tight, and I let the rush of emotions fall out of my eyes. I felt her squeeze me back and I cried harder. I missed this for so long, and for what? All of my anxieties and negative emotions brushed away in an instant. I had the power to do it all along if I had just given my wife the chance; if I had just let her in all this time.

"Babe," I was barely able to get that out between cautious sobs.

"Shhh," she said, as she gently pet the back of my head, still embracing me.

"Babe, I'm so sorry."

"Oh, don't be. I told you we'd get through this." She was so gentle with her words.

"I love you so much," I admitted.

That shocked even me. I knew what I was saying, but I never thought I'd say that to her ever again about ten minutes ago.

"I love you, too, baby. We're going to be OK." I knew she loved me; only someone who loved me as much as she did would hold a man in his weakest moments the way that she did.

Suddenly, Sea wasn't even a thought in my mind. The last thing I considered was that she really was just a figment of my subconscious, trying to coach me through all of the anxiety and all of the depression and all of the withdrawing. That was the only thing that made sense; there was no other way to explain how her kiss WAS my wife's kiss. I was smitten all over again.

We stood there for awhile, locked in each other's love. She would occasionally rub my back, and I just continued to sob on her shoulder. When the tears finally subsided, I held her face with her cheeks, kissed her a couple times on the lips, once on the forehead, and said, "Let's have this date, shall we?"

That beautiful smile came back on her face and she was back to shy, accepting my request with nothing more than a bashful nod.

The rest of the evening went tremendously: we sat and talked for hours, reminiscing as I assumed we would, catching up, just talking about the world. Anything and everything that came to our minds, we discussed; we ended up closing the place down. It was one of the best nights I'd had in I don't even remember when.

"I'm sorry to cut you short, but I'm afraid we're closing," apologized the waiter.

"It's already closing time?" I looked at my watch for confirmation. "Oh my God, I'm so sorry! Could we get our bill?"

"You know what?" My wife interrupted. "Hang on a second." She leaned over to grab her purse and went rifling through it. She gave it a look of confusion and went digging some more. The waiter and I looked at each other before she said, "Here it is!" She pulled something out and handed it to the waiter.

My confused look transferred from the waiter to my wife. "Just run it on that. We don't need to see the bill!" She smiled at the waiter and then shifted her glance to me. She rested her elbow on the table, and then in turn rested her chin into the pocket of her forefinger and thumb. She raised an eyebrow at me and then there it was; that devious Mona Lisa smile again.

My look of confusion shifted to satisfaction as I went through my thought process. I wondered what she gave the waiter, and then realized it was a credit card. But then I wondered where she got the credit card, and then I realized it was the credit card I had left at the bar.

"It was never Sea," I said to the table. I thought Sea had somehow come out of my dreams, into reality, and came by to get my card from the bar; it had been my wife all this time.

"What?" asked my wife, her smile fading.

I looked up at her and rephrased. "It was always you."

Her smile came back and she stared at me.

"It's always been you, babe," I smiled back. "But how did you know I was there to go get it?"

She collapsed her arms onto the table and crossed them. "Well, when I checked our bank account, I noticed a charge from the bar, so I went and did a little detective work. Apparently, you just walked out on your tab, so they ran the card."

"Yeah, about that…" I started. She threw up a hand and continued with her story.

"You don't have to say anything. I'm just glad you're ok. I was so worried with what was going on that I went up there. The bartender, that Cody guy, told me you kinda sat there like you were ready to fall asleep after your first drink and just, walked out the door."

"Yeah, I'm pretty sure I fell asleep while I was there and then drove home! You know how my sleepwalking can get."

"Like I said, I'm just glad you're OK," she said, and smiled at me. I smiled back and we had yet another moment of electricity.

Right before we left, we had our final staring contest. A lot less intense, a lot more passionate, and a lot more smiling in both directions.

I've said in the past that no matter what happens to us throughout our lives, we are responsible for our own happy endings. I was so scared that after what our marriage had dissolved into, that I would never get that. But this was my happy ending; she was it. I just got so consumed in myself that I didn't stop to realize that I was writing it out of my life; I was doing it to myself. That was why I couldn't stop staring at her before we left; I finally came to fruition that she was my happy ending.

20

"So, things are better for you now?" asked Sea. I eyed her for a minute, knowing full well that she knew the answer to that question.

"I think you already know," I replied.

"Humor me," she said, bearing my wife's smile again. A smile reflexively came across my own face.

"I've never been better," I explained. "Things are great with my wife, I've reestablished my relationship with my family, work is going great; I'm in a really great place right now."

"All great things to hear," she admitted. "Is there anything else you need from me?"

I pondered what she said for a minute, not sure if she was trying to get something out of me, or just making sure. "I think I'll be OK," I said finally. I outstretched my arms and took a step toward her. "May I?"

She made the same gesture and took a step toward me. We hugged each other in a gentle embrace, both carefully brushing the other's back.

"Thank you," I said, still wrapped up on her.

"For what?"

"For everything: for helping me see the light," I softly giggled. "For knocking some sense into me. For coaching me through my relationship. For everything."

"You did it all yourself," she claimed.

"Nah, I couldn't have done it without you. You're the reason I'm at where I am right now."

"So are you," she responded. I broke our tangle and took a step back.

"'So am I' what?" I asked.

"You're the reason I'm at where I am right now."

"What do you mean by that?"

She laughed. "You just won't rest until I tell you my story, huh?"

"Sure won't!" I retorted.

"In time," she consoled.

"Yeah, you keep saying that."

"In time," she repeated.

As though she had never existed before, she disappeared from the island instantly. Her presence itself ceased to linger among the air. I smiled to myself, as this was the final proof I needed that she wasn't existent; never was.

My hands found their way back into my pockets as I watched a colony of gulls fly overhead, their faint mewing was almost unheard against the sounds of the crashing waves. There was a clear sky with a wispy fluff of white markings the sky here and there. The giant orange fireball in the sky was still just peeking over the horizon, casting a mixed palette of reds, blues, violets, and oranges across the twilight sky. The greyscale no long existed, and the island was much more comfortable to exist in; much homier.

I walked toward the shoreline and watched rays of sunshine shimmer effortlessly across the water. I looked at the sand beneath me and squatted down into a catcher's pose. I found a rock sitting next to me, so I picked up and gently chucked it into the water. It skipped a couple times and disappeared. I let myself fall back and I sat on the ground, pulling my legs up to my chest and hugging them.

I stared out into the sun, reflecting on the beauty of this freshly vibrant island and it's juxtaposition with my reconstructed life. The peace I finally found within myself had manifested on this island and I could've stayed here forever, if I hadn't fallen back in love with my own life.

I pulled away from the view and looked at the sand to reflect on something that was still bothering me.

"There's something else on your mind," I heard a voice say.

She sure does have a gift. My gaze turned to her and I nodded dimly.

"What is it?" she wondered.

"I just," I hesitated for a minute. "I had a stroke awhile back; or at least I thought I did. The doctors claimed it wasn't a stroke, but they couldn't tell me what happened; they couldn't figure it out." I looked up at her. "Do you know what happened?"

Sea broke her glance and looked down at the ground herself. "I told you not to say anything."

"What?"

"I told you to keep me a secret and you didn't listen." I just stared at her; it was all I could do. "When you brought me up in that counseling session, I had to do something. I couldn't let you talk about me; everything would've come apart."

"So, you made me have a stroke?"

"No, just a defense mechanism. You just blacked out. Everything like a stroke, but harmless."

"How could you make that happen if you're just part of my subconscious?"

"Where did you come up with that?"

"What do you mean? That's the only thing that explains everything."

"It's not true."

"So, then, what are you?"

"In time…"

"No," I cut her off. "The time is now." We stared at each other hard. "Tell me."

"My past comes with a long story that I don't have time to tell right now."

"Then when will you tell me?"

She slowly stood up, turned away from me, and sauntered away in the direction the gulls were headed. She seemed to consider each step as she took them.

"You're never going to tell me, are you?" I shouted finally.

"I'll tell you," she called back over her shoulder.

"Yeah?" I asked. "When?" The tedious, obnoxious rhythm from an alarm clock began clouding my auditory senses.

"You're an impatient one."

"Well, I think you owe me at least that," I argued.

"What? Impatience?"

"You're story!"

"Owe you? I just gave you your life back!" The alarm clock was growing louder and started to grip my attention.

"Just tell me!" I begged.

"The next time we meet, you have my word that I'll tell you where I came from," she said finally.

And then I woke up.

Made in the USA
Lexington, KY
29 March 2017